Flannelmouth Finnegan

A young man's odyssey in urban America

by

Willard C. Richan

Flannelmouth Finnegan is a work of fiction. All
characters are fictional, and any similarity to persons
living or dead is purely coincidental.

ABOUT THE AUTHOR

Willard C. Richan is the author of *The Onion Man* (2010) and *Lobbying for Social Change* (2006), now in its third edition. He is a professor emeritus at Temple University. Since his retirement in 1993, he has been actively involved in educational and social issues in Chester, Pennsylvania, where he now makes his home. In the 1960s, Dr. Richan directed a research project that played a critical role in the federal court decision ordering the desegregation of the Cleveland, Ohio, public schools.

flan·nel·mouth.

–noun. **1.** a person whose speech is thick, slow, or halting.

2. a person whose speech is smoothly deceptive.

-Dictionary.com.

Chapter 1.

Still on the run.

He watches her kneeling by the stream, washing clothes. A beauty with long flowing hair. Fascinated, he creeps closer until he's only a few feet away. She appears not to see him, so engrossed is she in the task at hand. To his horror, he sees that the clothes she's washing are soaked in blood. Not clothes but a suit of armor.

She suddenly looks up like a frightened animal, and as she does so she turns into a horrible hag with gaps between her teeth. Out of her mouth comes a keening cry that soars into the night sky.

Flannelmouth was awake now. The keening cry continued. In the half-light he saw that it was coming from an odd contraption on the other side of the room. Furnace? Not like any he'd ever seen. It had a noisy motor that was working overtime. The motor wound down with a whine.

He was trying desperately to get his bearings. Where the hell was he? Oh yes, the priest. It all seemed like only yesterday. In point of fact, it was only yesterday....

The store clerk had grabbed him when he tried to scoot out past the end of the checkout counters with the cheese. Damn, nice Dubliner, too. Not like those English cheddars. Flannelmouth could usually talk his way out of things, but this store manager insisted on calling the cops.

Within hours our friend found himself sitting outside a courtroom with a matron next to him staring out the window. There were too many people around to make a break for it. So he sat there thinking of that Dubliner. Damn.

An old guy wearing a navy blue suit and a badge opened the door and beckoned him inside.

Big courtroom. Smelled of furniture polish. The guy in the blue suit was pushing him toward the front of the courtroom. Stop shoving, man, I'm going. The matron was right behind. Blue Suit nodded to Flannelmouth to sit down on a wooden bench up front.

There were a couple dozen people sitting around the room. Three lawyers were down front joking it up. You could always tell lawyers; suited up like it was a funeral and kidding around with the court staff.

The judge, who looked to be a hundred, was busy writing and looking at papers. Everybody else just sat and waited. A woman over to the left let out an audible sigh. The judge looked over at her, scowled, then went back to whatever he was doing.

Jesus, thought Flannelmouth, I knew court could take forever, but this is ridiculous. They must get paid by the hour and want to wrack up a pile of time. Well, they could wait? He could wait.

By now a priest was standing up front talking to the judge. He kept pointing over at a girl who looked like death's angel. They droned on and on.

Flannelmouth is sailing over the land chased by a big white dog that keeps trying to bite his rear end.

"Finnegan." It popped him awake.

Big conference down front with the matron. Then the judge looked out at Flannelmouth, who stared back. You don't scare me, judge. Been around this tour too many times before.

A nudge and a nod from Blue Suit and he was standing up in front of the judge. The old guy had deep wrinkles and little spaces between his front teeth. You could smell the bad breath from a couple yards away. The judge beckoned to the priest and waved him over.

Another big conference.

"But, you honor, I'm not...." Flannelmouth couldn't hear the rest. The priest looked unhappy. The judge looked ready to move on.

"O.K., Vernal," checking his notes, "says you stole a cheese in the supermarket. Yes or no? Did you?" He was glowering down at Flannelmouth.

"By all the saints in heaven, you honor, not to mention my dear mother departed these many years, do I look like somebody who would....?"

"They caught you carrying a cheese out of the market. Did you do it?"

Pause. "Yeah."

"Speak up, son, I'm hard of hearing."

"Yeah."

Why'd you go and do a thing like that, son?"

Flannelmouth thought for a while, then, "I like cheese. Hey, it's better than selling drugs."

There were guffaws in the courtroom. The judge banged his gavel, and they quieted down. The old man was clearly not pleased with the answer or the attitude.

"You know, I could send you right back to that training school you ran away from. Mecklenburg....Middleburg. I have a good mind to send you packing right out there."

No way was he going back to Middleburg. He'd kill himself first.

"Yessir." Flannelmouth was toning it down. Don't give the old geezer any excuses to send you back to that house from Hell.

The priest spoke up. "Your honor, Middleburg has a bad reputation. There was that fire in the isolation room last spring. A teenager died...."

"Yes, I know, father," said the judge, "took them ten minutes to find the key to the place. That and the brainwashing...."

"Behavior modification, I believe...."

"Yes, whatever." The judge didn't like to be corrected. He sat pondering things for a while, then, "O.K., father, looks like you have a choice. The good places are all booked up solid. Waiting lists and all. No regular foster home is going to take this kid. He's got a string of offenses as long as your arm. You have a choice, as I say. I turn the kid over to you or I send him back to Middleburg.'

The priest took a long time answering. Flannelmouth wished he could do mental telepathy. Come on father. You and me, huh, father? He was already figuring how he'd make his escape, once he got to the priest's place.

Deep breath. "All right."

"And make sure he gets to mass Sundays, father."

"But you honor, I'm not....."

The judge cut him off. "All right, son, you're going with Father..." -- looking down at his notes -- "...Morgan. And thank you, father." He handed the priest some papers. "Sign right there at the bottom."

Father Morgan put up his hand to protest, but the judge wasn't looking. There was more paperwork, and the clerk gave the father one of the papers and smiled.

The judge banged his gavel and said, "O.K. short recess," and he was up out of his chair and out the side door in no time.

Meanwhile, Flannelmouth was checking the guy out. A little on the chubby side. Hard to read the age. Good eyes. You could tell a lot by watching the eyes.

The priest came over to Flannelmouth. "Hi, Vernal, I'm Greg Morgan," and extended his hand. "Looks like you and I are stuck with each other for the time being at least." Not too happy with the thing, but he shot Flannelmouth a big smile. Trying to be friends? Forget it. Flannelmouth was having none of it. He finally reached out and shook the hand. Jesus, powerful grip.

"Let's go outside and talk." Father Morgan nodded toward the rear of the courtroom.

Once out in the waiting area, he sat Flannelmouth down on a bench and slid in next to him.

"O.K., so let's see. Vernal E. Finnegan," he said, reading from the paper they'd given him. "O.K., birthdate...uh-huh. Hmm, March 20th. By any chance is your middle name Equinox?"

The guy must be a wizard or something. "How'd you know that?"

"Oh, just a wild guess," said the other smiling.

"I don't do mass," Flannelmouth said. He waited for the reaction.

"If you mean the Catholic kind, neither do I," said the father.

Flannelmouth looked over at him. "What kind of a priest are you?"

"Episcopal. Judge Dornan is, let's just say, getting on in years. Any guy with the collar is of the faith as far as he's concerned. By the way, church is optional. Come on, I'm going to get you set up so you have a place to sleep."

The trip to St. Luke's was something of a blur. Nobody had much to say on the way. As the father pulled up next to the old brick building, he nodded over his shoulder. "O.K., get your bag. I'll show you where you're going to be staying while we work out a permanent arrangement for you."

Instead of going around to the main entrance, he took Flannelmouth along a concrete walkway and down a flight of metal steps to a red basement door.

"Here, hold these," he said, handing Flannelmouth a sheaf of papers, including the order they'd given him at the court. Out came a keyring, and he quickly unlocked the door. He took Flannelmouth inside. "I'll get you a key so you can let yourself in if you need to. See, you turn toward the door casing to unlock it, away from it to lock."

Flannelmouth nodded. No locks? No guards? He could zip out of there any time he wanted to. Maybe the fact that he could bolt the place so easily made it less urgent to do so.

They were now in a corridor that ran the length of the building. Nodding to a closed door on the left, "This is my room. Off limits, of course." Flannelmouth nodded.

Next to it was a big side room with long tables across the center and dozens of folding chairs up against the wall.

"This is the heart of the operation," said Father Greg. "We do food cupboard and law clinic and community meetings here."

What kind of a church was this? Well, the old man had always said the protties were strange ducks. The way he said it, you knew it was something you didn't want to be. It always caused a lot of trouble with the mother's family -- old line protties from way back.

Father Morgan waved a hand in the direction of a row of smaller rooms to the right. "Used to be Sunday school classrooms. That one has a TV and an easy chair and some books. We use it as a lounge. The one after that is where we'll put you up." All Flannelmouth could see inside that room was a folding chair and a table. The father answered his unasked question with a chuckle. "No, you won't have to sleep on the table. We'll get the place fixed up. For now you'll be down at the end of the hall. I'll show you in a minute." Flannelmouth could only imagine what lurked behind the closed door at the end of the corridor.

On their left as they proceeded along was what looked like a storeroom and a large kitchen just beyond.

Not a bad looking kitchen. Beyond that was a flight of stairs and a bathroom with a plastic shower stall in the corner.

"This is where you'll be for now," as he opened the door at the end of the corridor. A single bulb overhead revealed a cot and an orange crate next to it. Flannelmouth was used to roughing it.

So that's how the rest of the day went. The father made them spaghetti and meatballs and salad for supper. Flannelmouth skipped the salad.   Canned peaches for dessert. He was still thinking about that Dubliner.

After dinner, more TV -- at least there were movies and sitcoms. Father Greg was an early to bed early to rise type, so it wasn't long before Flannelmouth was down for the night.

That was all before.

*

Flannelmouth lay there on the cot in the semi-darkness. The wind machine started up again with its keening wail. Were they trying to spook him out of his wits? Torture, that's what it was. The judge had sentenced him to live in the torture chamber forever, listening to the awful sound. He drifted off back to sleep.

Lots of old men with hooded white robes and long beards were standing in a big circle. Around the outside you could see huge stones standing up on end with other stones across them like bridges. The men were chanting some nonsense and walking around the circle.

He knew they were telling him something but he couldn't make out what it was.

Back awake again. The wind machine still doing its torture routine. Flannelmouth wanted most of all to get away from the racket. He noticed a flight of stairs to one side, leading up to a door at the top. Why not? He threw on his clothes and went to investigate.

As he got near the top of the stairs, he heard what sounded like music. He tried the door. As it swung open, he was hit by a big blast of music, and he found himself staring at the wide backside of a lady playing an organ. Up against the wall in front of her were rows of pipes going up to the ceiling. He could see he was up at the business end of a church. The altar and a huge hanging cross were to his left and two lecterns to his right. Two women were down in the pews straightening up.

The lady at the organ stopped playing, swung around, caught a glimpse of Flannelmouth, and just stared.

"Who are you?" she finally said.

"I was sleeping. The father put me in the furnace room down there," and he gestured toward the door he had just emerged from.

The lady looked like she'd just seen St. Patrick's ghost. "Mrs. Simpson! Where's Father Morgan?"

By then the two other ladies had come to the front and were gaping at Flannelmouth. One of them half walked, half ran up the aisle toward the rear yelling, "I'll get him! Just a minute."

Flannelmouth stood taking it all in. Best thing to do when you don't know what's going on. Pretty soon here comes the lady with Father Greg at her heels.

"Hi, Vernal," he said like he was chatting about the weather, "have a good sleep?"

"Yeah, except for the noise in that furnace thing."

The ladies didn't say peep.

"Oh that, hah, hah. That's the organ bellows. Motor pumps them up. Mrs. Gantry there was practicing for tomorrow's service. The furnace is in another room behind."

"Sounded more like somebody just died and the old women in black were doing their keening routine," said Flannelmouth.

"Oh, excuse me, ladies," said the father, "this is Vernal Finnegan. He's going to be staying with us for a while." Turning to Flannelmouth, "This is Mrs. Simpson and Miss Montague," nodding toward the two ladies down front.

The ladies nodded back with funny looks on their faces, like they were used to the guy doing strange things.

"Come on, Vernal, we'll get you some breakfast," said the father.

The two of them headed down to the kitchen by way of the front stairs, with the women cluck-clucking in their wake. O.K., father, you and me.

Flannelmouth sat at the kitchen table and watched the show.

"Cereal? We got several kinds, Vernal. Fruit Loops? Got raisin bran somewhere here." Father Greg opened the cupboard door and showed his wares.

Flannelmouth shrugged.

"Raisin bran? That's better than those sugary things."

"Raisin bran's O.K." Then, "I don't use Vernal. People call me Flannelmouth."

"Flannelmouth Finnegan. What a great name. Like Huckleberry Finn sort of. How'd you get that monicker?"

"First grade teacher gave it to me. I tripped on my way to school one day and went down in a heap. Bit my tongue real bad. I can still feel it. By the time I got to school, my tongue must have been swelled up to twice its size. The teacher said I sounded like I had a mouth full of flannel. That's why she called me 'Flannelmouth.' Been that way ever since. I don't mind. Sure beats Vernal."

Father Greg laughed. "Take a spoon from the cup there.... No, we got soup spoons.... Yeah, that works better with cereal." The father was getting a bowl down from the shelf and filling it with cereal as he talked.

"The judge said you're in the seventh grade. How old are you?"

"Fourteen. I got left behind once or twice."

"That's O.K., I'm not trying to grill you. How about orange juice?" and he brought a carton of juice out of the refrigerator along with a container of milk.

Flannelmouth liked orange juice. This was the real stuff. Middleburg used to water the juice or else give them those little plastic jars with colored sugar water and call it juice.

"I was slow in school," said the father as Flannelmouth munched on his breakfast. "Dyslexic. Still takes me a long time to read something. But you find ways. I was bright enough, just the reading. It's something in the brain. I bet you're smart. Ever been tested?"

Flannelmouth thought. "Yeah, but I don't remember when."

"Maybe we can set up some testing. Uncover your true potential."

Flannelmouth sat looking at him. "My true what?"

The reverend laughed. "See what kind of talents you got in there," and he pointed in the general direction of Flannelmouth's forehead. "You had to have brains to have survived this long."

Guy was O.K. But what was he doing hanging out in a church basement?

"How come you live here in the church?" Might as well ask right out.

"Ah, well, St. Luke's has been going through some hard times. Most of the congregation switched to churches in the 'burbs because of the changing neighborhood. The diocese decided it had to sell off the parsonage to break even. That did it for the former pastor. He had a family with kids. Didn't want to bring them up in a church basement, I guess. If you come to church tomorrow, you'll see what I mean. A few oldsters still hanging in there."

Flannelmouth was getting more than he'd asked for. It was obvious he'd hit a tender nerve with the father.

"How's your Spanish, Ver... Flannelmouth?"

"I just speak English."

"We'll try to arrange for you to learn a little street talk. Comes in handy around here."

"I know a few Gaelic words," said Flannelmouth, trying to be helpful.

"O.K., that could be interesting," said Father Morgan. "I don't know any Gaelic. How do you say, 'Welcome to St. Luke's in Gaelic?"

"*Aon, do, tri, ceathair....*"

"That means welcome?"

"That's counting," said Flannelmouth. "I don't know how you say welcome."

The father laughed. "*Bienvenido.* That's 'welcome' in Spanish. Or *Que tal*? That's 'How goes it?'"

Flannelmouth could see Spanish was not going to be easy. He was about done with the cereal, and Father Greg said, "Want anything else? Toast? We got eggs in the fridge."

"No, this is O.K."

"So what happened back there at the supermarket?"

Oh? Different topic. Flannelmouth struggled to pick up the beat.

"I swear, I don't know, father. I think I blacked out for a while. You know, people black out sometimes. It's been that way since my dear mother died."

"And when was that?"

Flannelmouth thought for a moment. The guy would check it out. "I was three they say."

"Three. And you've been blacking out ever since, right?"

Flannelmouth nodded.

"Like when somebody catches you taking something?"

No point in screwing around. He shrugged. "I grabbed a cheese and they grabbed me."

"Just like that."

"Just like that," said Flannelmouth.

"You got a family? Father, stepmother, brothers and sisters?"

Here we go again, thought Flannelmouth. "Mother died in childbirth when I was three years old. Baby girl was adopted out. Old man took over, but he and I have had it. He's got a little drinking problem, you might say. Me? Been in and out of homes since then. I get by O.K." He spilled it out like a machine.

The father was shaking his head. "So how'd you land in Middleburg?"

"Incorrigible." Flannelmouth knew all the terminology.

"Oh, like what?"

He took his time answering. "Missed school a few times. Got in fights -- just defending myself, you understand."

"Of course. You had nothing to do with it, right? Or were you just standing up to the bullies?"

"Something like that."

"And the shoplifting? Things just find their way into your pockets?"

"Just food mostly. I'd of starved otherwise."

"Of course. Anything besides food?"

"Oh never. I'm not like a regular shoplifter, you understand."

"I'm beginning to," said the other. "Uh, O.K., so how come you left Middleburg?"

"That place was bad news. You and the judge said so yourselves. It was easy getting out of there."

"And when was that?"

"Couple weeks ago. Been hanging out in somebody's garage since then. Kid let me use it. His folks were off to their summer place. Older sister in charge. They let me use the bathroom inside. Sister was cool with that."

More head shakes from the father. "What did you do for food?"

"They kept me with the necessaries."

"Plus a few trips to supermarkets for cheese and stuff like that?"

"Yeah. Small corner grocers are better. Nobody watching most of the time. Look, I just take what I have to to keep going. I'm not a thief, if you know what I mean. Nothing valuable. I know guys who...."

"I'm sure you do." Another pause. "O.K.," said the priest. "We'll see about getting you a more permanent set up. Meanwhile, you'll stay here with me. You've got to watch yourself. I have no time for nonsense. I live here, too, you know. You're welcome to eat anything here in the kitchen. We also keep the place spotless, which you will be expected to do, too. Keep your mitts off the storeroom back there, as well as anything else around the church. Any funny business, and it's right back to court. And I'm assuming that means right back to Middleburg. Do we understand each other?"

Under the clerical collar and the innocent blue eyes was a tough customer. Those blue eyes could look right through you and come out the other side.

"Yes." Flannelmouth was trying to get his head around the whole thing.

Father Greg reached out, and they shook hands. Done deal, apparently.

"O.K., milk and juice go in the fridge. Wash your dishes and put them upside down in the basket. We don't wipe them -- makes more germs. Then do your teeth, et cetera. You'll find a toothbrush in a plastic envelope by the sink. Then I'm going to take you on a little tour of the neighborhood."

As Flannelmouth was on his way back from the bathroom, there was a clatter at the end of the corridor. Couple of foreign looking ladies carrying cartons and jabbering away in Spanish. They gave Flannelmouth a smile and a nod and went into the kitchen. He could hear them and the father rattling away in Spanish.

Later he and Father Greg were on their way out the door, and he asked about the Spanish ladies.

"They're with the Adventists. Bringing in refreshments. They hold church service Saturday afternoons," said the father. "We let them use the church. They're working on a building fund to put up their own church."

The neighborhood was like a dozen Flannelmouth had seen in his life, one block like a row of rotting teeth with junk-filled cavities where houses had once stood.

The next showing signs of new life, with plants struggling up in the center of old truck tires next to the sidewalk and cheap metal awnings jutting out over the fronts. And, just beyond, a row of three- and four-story apartment buildings, some boarded up, all in bad shape. A vacant corner lot turned into a weed field; Flannelmouth tried to imagine what it had looked like when there were buildings there. A few *bodega* signs; a travel agency/insurance company; one burned out hulk with weeds growing out of the basement windows. Cars of various ages and conditions were parked along the curb. Bar facing into one corner with a few people going in and out. Not many folks out at this hour. Most looked Spanish. One or two colored folks.

"Place is called Cedarwood," said the father. "If there are any cedars around her, I haven't seen them. Name was no doubt some realtor's creation back in the early twentieth century when this was prime real estate."

Flannelmouth had heard the name before, but that was all he knew. Father Greg pointed out this place and that place, most of which Flannelmouth would soon forget. No matter. He'd be out of here as soon as the father could line up a place for him to stay. Maybe with luck, before then. He was used to shifting around.

The thing that struck him was the way everybody knew the guy. And he knew them. Sometimes it was a "When's the law clinic, reverend? Tuesday? O.K., seven o'clock, right?"

"You got it, Sam. How's you're daughter doing, by the way? Welfare still giving her a hard time?"

Sometimes it was in Spanish. Who new what that was about?

It took them a good quarter hour just to make it down to the next block. Each time they met somebody, the father would say something like, "This is my friend Flannelmouth Finnegan.... No, Flannelmouth. Yeah, you got it."

In between he'd explain who he'd just been talking to. Guy ought to run for senator or something. Flannelmouth had seen politicians working the streets before, but you knew it was phony. This guy really connected.

Later, back in the church basement, Father Greg said, "Look, I have to get ready for church tomorrow. You can watch TV, O.K.? Stay out of the way when the folks come in for their church service, O.K.?"

"Er, the key, father?"

"Oh, yeah. Wait a minute." He ducked into his room and in a minute came out and handed Flannelmouth the key. "Now put that in a safe place and don't lose it," he said.

Oh, indeed, father, I'll be sure not to. Then, "Oh, I got to get something," heading down the hall toward his temporary quarters as he spoke. Once inside, he closed the door and, with a quickness born of long experience, pulled out his clothes and stuffed them into the laundry bag marked 'Middleburg.' In the middle he stopped, dumped the clothes out, turned the bag inside out, and crammed the clothes back in. O.K., no Middleburg. The door to Father Greg's room was closed. A couple seconds' look up and down the hall told Flannelmouth the coast was clear. Out the door at the end he went, up the metal steps and off to who knew where? Certainly not Flannelmouth Finnegan.

Chapter 2.

The prodigal returns to the fold.

He kept to streets where he and the father had not walked earlier. Same rundown feel to the place. On the cross street up ahead he saw lots of traffic going by. Safer there. In no time he was dodging in and around shoppers, deftly shifting his bag of clothes from side to side to avoid collisions. Not too fast. Nothing to attract attention. Not that anybody paid any attention to a fourteen-year-old kid minding his own business. Too involved in their own affairs.

Food. One thing Flannelmouth Finnegan had was an appetite. You wouldn't guess it from the looks of him. But now nature told him it was time for lunch. Like a rat, he'd eat anything in sight, except he went for quality when it was within range. Stay away from the food carts. Those folks had eyes in the backs of their heads. More than once he'd been caught swiping something off a curbside stand, and right now he wasn't about to risk being caught by anybody. Besides, the bag of clothes would slow him down if he had to run.

Instead, he checked out the stores with food displays on the sidewalk. Vegetable stand outside a store across the street was perfect. Kids were not known for eating vegetables. Being a white kid didn't hurt, either.

He stood watching the traffic in and out of the store for a long time. When an old guy with an apron came out and headed up the street, he figured it was the boss going to lunch.

Flannelmouth went to the intersection, crossed over and walked down the sidewalk at a leisurely pace. He loosened the neck of the bag as he went. When he got to the stand, he took a quick look around, then grabbed a bag of string beans and a couple of tomatoes and stuffed them into the sack. Better than nothing. He'd go hunting for a pie or muffin or something later. Don't run. Take your time. He stood around looking out at the traffic for a while, then sauntered along the street.

Around the next corner, he made for a church halfway up the block with steps leading up to the front door. Settling down on the top step, he wiggled a couple times to make himself comfortable, sat looking around for half a minute, then went to work on the veggies.

Flannelmouth had style. First out of the sack came a tomato, and down it went on the step just so. The second tomato next to it. No, a mite further over on the step. There, just right. Now out came the bag of string beans. He held it up and scanned the contents through the plastic as it rotated in his hand. Oh that cheat! Rotten beans under the good ones. Man ought to be put out of business, offering such crummy wares to an unsuspecting public. Flannelmouth's sense of morality at work.

He was about to take a bite out of the first tomato when he spied the two big black guys going by. Out of instinct he froze in place, hoping they would miss him. No such luck. The one with a baseball cap draped over his left ear nudged his buddy and whispered something. Pretty soon they were right up next to Flannelmouth.

"Yo, man, what you doin' in my block?"

Flannelmouth shrugged and nodded toward the groceries. His hand tightened on the bag of clothes just a bit.

"Hey, dude, lunch time, huh?" He was the one you had to watch. Didn't take his eyes off Flannelmouth. The other kept checking out his buddy to see what the next play was.

The boss man reached down and picked up the second tomato. "Here, catch," he said to the other, who made a clumsy attempt to grab it. The tomato went bouncing down the steps and into the middle of the sidewalk with a splat. That sent the two of them into a laughing fit.

"What you name, man?"

"Finnegan." Flannelmouth knew enough to keep it low, cool, but not sassy.

"Finnegan? Hey, Crimmy, you hear that? This here is Finnegan."

He pointed at the bag. "What's in there, Finnegan?"

"Dirty laundry." Flannelmouth was intent on rescuing the bag with 'Middleburg' printed on the inside. They could have the clothes. He'd figure a way to get more.

Boss man grabbed the bag and began turning it different ways. Then he turned it upside down and let the clothes fall out onto the steps, watching Flannelmouth for a reaction. He kicked the clothes down the steps, then tossed the bag in the general direction of our friend.

"Get your white ass out of my block, dude. This here is enemy territory as far as you're concerned. Dig?"

Flannelmouth knew the rules in this kind of game. He shrugged, grabbed the bag and took off down the steps while the other two began tossing the green beans at each other. He didn't look back until he got a few doors away from the church. By then the two black guys were already halfway down the block. Flannelmouth ran back, quickly stuffed his clothes in the bag, and was soon off up the street toward the main drag.

In rich Irish metaphor, he brought down every curse he knew on the heads of the two who had spoiled his meal. It didn't matter that they were long gone and oblivious to the fate he was visiting on them -- perhaps no worse than in reality what awaited them in the dark streets. The purpose of curses -- especially those uttered in absentia -- is, after all, not to punish the other but to salve the injured pride of the one who curses.

The more immediate issue was that the curses were not going to get Flannelmouth the lunch his body so desperately craved. He thought about hitting another market but then had a better idea: If he made it back to St. Luke's before Father Greg finished writing his sermon, Flannelmouth could pretend he'd been watching TV all this time. What's that, father? Did I have lunch already? Oh no, sir, I was waiting for you.

One of the lad's many survival skills was an unerring sense of direction, no matter the place he landed, and he soon rounded the corner and saw St. Luke's up ahead. O blessed sanctuary, the refuge of the soul and source of spiritual sustenance. More to the point at the moment was sustenance of a more earthly kind.

As he clattered down the metal steps and unlocked the basement door, he heard singing and knew the Adventist service was in full swing. The door to the Father Morgan's room was ajar, but he was nowhere to be seen.

Flannelmouth stepped into his temporary quarters and dumped his clothes on the bed. Just then Father Greg showed up in the doorway.

"Where were you?" he asked.

"Oh, out looking over the neighborhood, sir. I'm wanting to wash my clothes here."

"Right, I forgot to show you the laundry room. Right this way."

Good. The father was busy apologizing, so he wouldn't grill our young friend about his travels. But Flannelmouth's stomach was singing a different tune. O.K., father, let's see the laundry but then let's get to the kitchen.

As if reading the lad's mind, Father Greg stopped and said, "Hey, it's after two. You eat yet?"

"No, father, I was waiting for you."

"Oh, God, Flannelmouth, I'm sorry. I was so busy with the sermon I didn't think to check."

Flannelmouth let the apology go by.

They were well into the sandwiches when Father Morgan said, "So where were you headed?"

"Oh, Father, I don't know where I would have ended up if you hadn't brought me here."

"No, I mean just now -- when you took off with all your clothes."

"Oh, well, uh...."

"So I'm curious. Just kind of striking out for parts unknown? You can't keep running, Flannelmouth."

"Yeah, well, I, uh, got over on Juniper the other side of 14th. Church over there."

"Oh, you were over the line then." Father real calm.

"The line?"

"Yeah, you were in N-town."

"N-town?"

"I don't use the N word."

"I was in Niggertown?"

"Yep. Folks over this way generally don't go there and they stay out of here pretty much. I'm one of the few people around that can hang out in both places. Sometimes police cruisers drop off a kid from here on a street corner over there or vice versa. Blood sport for the cops, you might say."

Flannelmouth's jaw was hanging open. "Oh." So how did the padre know he'd taken off with his stuff? Jesus, got to watch this guy.

"You don't have to be here," said the reverend. "I'm sure they got a few vacant beds in Middleburg. Come Monday, we're going to try to get you set up somewhere. Until then, stick around. And if you want to explore N-town, you better take me along with you. Wouldn't be a bad idea, actually. Broaden your horizons a little bit."

No way would he go near N-town. He'd heard too many stories about guys getting beat up or killed even.

At Middleburg the colored kids stayed by themselves mostly. They slept in a different unit. This one guy -- Duane Bishop -- was different. He was cool. Shorter than most of them. Spent a lot of time putting his hair in tight braids. Lots of smiles.

Flannelmouth and Duane got put on dish detail after breakfast one time. Pots and pans. Oatmeal caked on like cement. It meant they were stuck there after everybody else was gone from the place.

"Sheeh," said Duane, "take a Uzi to blast this shit off."

Flannelmouth didn't say anything. Never up that close to a colored kid before.

"Where you from?" asked Duane.

"All over. Other side of the city. Asbury mostly. How about you?"

"Asbury a mean place. My old man got arrested for doin' nothin' over there. Me, I'm from South Side. You know South Side?"

"Yeah. Well, I mean, I know about it. Never been there."

"Then how you know 'bout it, man?" Not angry. Duane was smiling.

"Well, yeah. O.K. You know, you hear stuff. You know...."

"So what you in for?" Duane was ready to change the subject. "By the way, we ought to get on the pots. Look that way anyway. Old Raymond come 'round, you got to look busy."

They went back to scouring. No talk for a while. Flannelmouth was beginning to see pot under the crud.

"So what they get you on?" Duane was looking at his pot.

"Incorrigible."

"Incorri what?"

"Means I screwed around in school, missed a lot of days. Fights. You know. Tried me in a few foster homes." Flannelmouth shrugged.

"I got in with some bigger guys," said Duane. "They passin' drugs. Had us breakin' into places. They was tried as adults and now they're doin' time. I mean real time, not this shit." It was all said in a matter-of-fact way, like what could you expect?

"You said about your old man," said Flannelmouth. "You got a family?"

"My mom, mainly. Old man's in and out. What about you?"

"My mom's dead. Old man supposed to be raising me, but I'm sort of on my own."

They went back to scouring. Duane held up his pot. "Race ya," he said. They went at it in earnest. Just then Raymond walked in, saw they were really working. "Hurry up, you guys. Got to get to class." He turned and walked out.

"Whew," said Duane, "Close one. That cat can be mean."

The only sound after that was Brillo on steel. Flannelmouth finally finished his pot and looked over. Duane was standing there smiling with his own pot all done.

After that Flannelmouth and Duane hung out together a lot. Duane was in a different unit. He said the older black guys told him he ought to stay with his own kind. "Sheeh, I don't pay them no mind," said Duane.

When Flannelmouth lit out of Middleburg, he didn't tell Duane he was going. In a way he wished he had. He wondered what happened to his friend. It was like that. See people, get to know them a little, then they go or you go, and you never see them again.

This place? He'd bide his time for a while, then try again.

Chapter 3.

Church and state arrive at a solution.

Father Greg -- that's what he wanted to be called -- was holding a letter and reading it over. "Hm, O.K. 'Pat Spetrino.' Looks like you got yourself a P.O., Flannelmouth."

The other munched on his raisin bran. So big deal. He'd con the guy enough so he'd leave him alone.

"He's supposed to come this morning. Maybe he can get you a permanent place to stay. So don't go wandering around the neighborhood, O.K.?"

Flannelmouth nodded and mumbled through his cereal.

A short while later, our young friend was struggling to stay focused on the page in front of him. He was losing the struggle.

He's sitting in the middle of a clearing in the woods, stuck to the ground. Little green leprechauns poking him with sticks, saying they've got to get the devil out of him. He keeps trying to get up, but he's stuck fast.

"Flannelmouth? Come on, boy, get to it." Father Greg was standing over him. Several pages of the book in front of him had flipped over, and he had no idea where he was supposed to be. English literature. Yes indeed, fascinating subject. No question about it.

"Oh yes, Father. It's a wonderful book. It got me thinking. You know, lost in thought I guess."

"Oh yes. Dreaming wonderful dreams no doubt. You got another half hour on this, then a break and we do math. Hey, where are your notes? Nice picture of a car, but that thing is for notes on what you're reading." He pulled the notebook over in front of Flannelmouth.

"Hello." Woman's voice from the stairwell.

"Hello," said Father Greg, "in here." He went to the door and looked up the corridor.

Then he backed away a little, and a short, thin woman with black hair and heavy eyebrows came into view. She put her hand out. Father Greg reached out and shook it automatically.

"Hi, I'm Pat Spetrino. Did you get my letter?"

The father said, "Oh, but I thought...."

"*Mr.* Spetrino? Yeah, people usually assume the P.O.s for the guys are male. New day out there, father."

She turned to Flannelmouth, still sitting and staring. Her hand shot out and he found himself shaking it. Tight grip. Tight lady. Flannelmouth checked out the eyes. They were all over the place, like she was doing you and everything around you at the same time.

"Can I get you a cup of coffee?" Father Greg was sort of smiling but not exactly.

"Sure, black is good," and the lady Pat looked around to see where it might pop out from. The father went to the fridge and took out a jar of instant. Ms. Pat gave a little nod and a raise of the eyebrows as if to say, "Oh well, we're not exactly Starbucks, are we?"

Father Greg fussed around with the microwave while the lady scanned the kitchen. The mouth, closed tight, was working overtime.

"You're Episcopal, right?"

"Yeah. Judge Dornan...."

"I know. Should have been retired ten years ago. Well, we got to do something about that -- unless of course you want to take the kid to mass every Sunday, which I assume you don't."

A nod from the father. "The other day I started calling around...."

"No need, father, that's part of my job." She took a small sip from the mug that had been set down in front of her and winced. "In the meantime, let's see how you got Vernal set up here."

"Oh, incidentally, he doesn't like Vernal. He likes to be called Flannelmouth." Father Morgan looked over at the lad, who nodded. Flannelmouth didn't utter a word.

A grin spread over the lady's face. "Flannelmouth? Where'd that come from?"

"It was a first grade teacher, ma'am. She called me that, and it's been like that ever since." At least now he was part of the conversation.

"Oh?" Nodding like it was taking her a minute to absorb this news. "O.K., neat. O.K., Flannelmouth," chuckling. "Why don't you show me around your digs? No, that's O.K., father, you stay put. I want some time with Flannelmouth anyway." She gave the boy a little nod as if to say, "Lead on."

Flannelmouth took her to his room and opened the door. She stepped in and took a quick look around, shaking her head. Looked like the room didn't pass inspection.

"I try to keep it neat in here, ma'am."

"That's not the problem, kid." There was an unspoken mutter on her mouth. "Where's the bathroom? You got a bathroom, I trust."

"Right this way, ma'am." Flannelmouth led her across the corridor to the bathroom.

"That a shower in the corner there?"

Sounding as if she didn't like anything about the place. Once they were out in the corridor again, "Where's the father's bathroom."

Flannelmouth nodded back where they had just come from. Up went her eyes and down came her jaw. Big sigh. Flannelmouth was beginning to sympathize with the father. Hell, it's not all that bad.

"C'mon," she said and headed back toward the kitchen. She'd said she wanted to talk to Father Greg. Looked like the agenda had changed.

Once they were back sitting around the kitchen table, Father Greg said, "More coffee?"

She ignored the invitation. "We gotta get this kid out of here, reverend. You're like breaking every rule in the book. If I let this kid stay here, they'll have my backside in the proverbial sling. Know what I mean?"

"Now just a minute, Pat -- it's Pat, right?" Different side of the father, one Flannelmouth hadn't seen before. "This may not be a great place, I'll admit, but...."

"Be in touch," and she was headed out the kitchen door.

"Here, I'll...." He got up and started to follow her out.

"Don't bother. I can find my way out."

Gone. But of course she'd be back. Back to yank Flannelmouth out of one more stopping place in an endless series of stopping places that had defined his life.

"Stupid bastards!" Definitely a different side of Father Greg. He slumped back into the kitchen chair and aimlessly twiddled the spoon in the cold coffee.

Then and there, our Flannelmouth made a decision. By hook or by crook, he was determined to stay put. You and me, father.

'Be in touch' didn't take more than a couple of days. The call came while Flannelmouth was trying to crank up some interest in Jonathan Swift. ("You ought to like this one; it's really about the Irish. You know, satire. You know he's not really talking about tiny people. That could be your ancestors in there." Good try, father.)

They were in Father Greg's upstairs office, Flannelmouth slouching on the couch with the book propped up in front of him and Father Greg at the computer. The phone jarred them both a little. The father stopped typing and picked up the phone. It was easy to tell who was on the other end.

"Oh, uh-huh, I see. Well, foster homes are pretty...uh-huh...yes, I understand...well, what about across the river maybe?.... Oh, different state. Yes, well that would...uh-huh...."

The father was shaking his head. "No, I really can't see a place like that for him.... I understand, yes I...uh-huh.... Look, I don't think we should be trying to decide something like this over the phone. Why don't you...? I understand.... A hundred and eighty-three? Wow, that's a lot of cases. You must really...yes, granted. But this kid has talent. Yes, I know, they're all special...."

Flannelmouth was having a hard time focusing on the Lilliputians while his fate was being decided.

"You say Tuesday is a field day up this way? O.K., how about next Tuesday?.... Afternoon is fine. Say about.... No, we have our adult literacy then. Could we make it 1:30?.... Two? O.K., see you then."

Father Greg clicked off the phone and dropped it on the cradle. "God, they don't make it easy." Talking to himself.

Hi, father, I'm over here. You wouldn't be talking about me by any chance, would you?

The telepathy worked. "Oh, yeah. Flannelmouth, my friend, Pat Spetrino is going to be coming by Tuesday, about...."

"Two. Yes, I heard."

"Oh, right. Sorry, old buddy. Sort of leaving you out of the mix, aren't we? Listen, you gotta swear on a stack of bibles not to do any more trips to the neighborhood between now and then. That's all they'd need to pack you off to God knows where."

"Oh, you have my word, father. I wouldn't think of...."

"Yes, I know. Just don't do it, period."

Flannelmouth nodded. He could always run later if things headed in the wrong direction. For now he'd sit tight and see what happened. For maybe the first time in his life, he didn't want to run.

"Now they're talking county children's home. Not good, my friend. Ever since the cutbacks, that place has been going downhill. There are foster home agencies won't touch you, apparently. Let's just say your reputation precedes you and then some. Oh well, can't go back and redo history. O.K., back to the studies."

Flannelmouth checked in on old Gulliver. Plenty of pictures along with the words. Good thing, because reading wasn't exactly Flannelmouth's strong suit. The man was roped down with stakes holding the ropes. The little people had him down but good. Flannelmouth could identify with that.

Tuesday was one of those drizzly late spring days when it just hangs, and the rain threatens to come pelting down any minute. Two o'clock came and went and no Lady Pat. About 2:25 the buzzer rang and they went to let her in.

Not just the lady. She had an old geezer in tow. Clerical collar. Pat was a little out of breath. "Sorry, we got tied up in traffic. It's raining pretty hard in some parts of the area. That always slows things up."

"That's O.K.," said Father Greg. "Need a minute to catch the breath?" Meanwhile he was checking out the other padre.

"Oh, excuse me, this is Father Morrissey. Father Morrissey, this is Reverend -- uh, Father -- Morgan."

"Hello, father." said Father Morrissey as they shook hands. "Fine church you have here. Maybe you can give me a tour before we leave." Hard to read. Flannelmouth was doing his usual eye check. Got to watch those friendly types. Never know what they're thinking.

Flannelmouth coughed.

"Oh, and this is the young man I was telling you about," said the lady. "Vernal Finnegan. He prefers to be called...."

"Ah, a fine Irish name there, young man." The tone and the look said Father Morrissey was used to taking charge.

"Father Morrissey is with the Catholic diocese," said Pat, "He was interested in meeting Flannelmouth."

Father Morrissey's eyes popped a little at the name, but then went back to their friendly twinkle.

"Yes, I've heard of you, Father Morrissey," said Father Greg. "You used to be at a church up in Linwood if I'm not mistaken."

"Oh, that was a good many years ago, son." Father Morrissey's eyes were shifting around a little. So nice to hear Father Greg referred to as son.

"I've been at the diocesan office for 12 years," said Father M. "It just got too much to -- uh...." and the rest sort of trailed off. Father M's eyes were shifting around a little more.

"Well," said Pat, "can we sit and talk somewhere?"

"Why don't we go upstairs to my office?" said Father Greg. He led the way up to the office, and people arranged themselves around the conference table in the middle. Flannelmouth sat down on a folding chair at the far corner of the table and tried to think how a fly on the wall would look. A small and inconspicuous fly.

Nobody was paying much attention anyway. Good, Flannelmouth liked it that way.

"Well, uh....," said Father Greg after everybody had settled in. So...."

Pat picked up the ball from there. "We really appreciate your stepping into the breach this way, father. But, well, it's what we talked about. The kid here needs to get moved to a more suitable environment. You know, it's not just the religious training and all, though that's important." She looked over at Father Morrissey as she said that last, and he nodded sagely.

Flannelmouth checked out Father Greg. Nothing. Just sat there listening. Poker face. Come on, father. Flannelmouth could see himself being shipped off to the county children's home.

Everybody was looking at Father Morrissey. He was looking off into space. "Well, yes, we must be sure our children get proper care." Hard to read the eyes now. Something was different. Meanwhile, Father Greg sat there cool and collected. Looked as if he had something up his sleeve.

Flannelmouth jumped in, and everybody else jumped back a little. "Ma'am, I was wondering, like, what the particulars are. I mean, could you break down what the state or the county or, you know, the people that put together that manual say a place should have."

"Well, uh, it's very detailed, you know. Pages and pages. Very detailed, you know."

"I was thinking," said Flannelmouth, "if we could make a list of things that a place needs, we could see if this place could be fixed up. Don't know whether the state or somebody could help with that sort of thing.

And, oh, father," looking over at Father Morrissey, "I do miss the mass, you know. Been a long time since I was to church. The priest used to come to Middleburg and hold mass -- Father Traverse -- nice man -- but it wasn't like being right there in church with the music and all."

He did a quick check. Ms. Pat was staring at her notebook. Father Morrissey was cocking his head. Got his attention at least. Father Greg, is that a smile? Hard to tell at this distance.

Pat said, "I don't know, I'll have to check with my supervisor. There are so many things here, the bathroom arrangement for instance."

"Tell you what," said Father Greg, "why don't Father Morrissey and I look at the set-up here? Maybe he and I can figure out something for getting Flannelmouth to mass on Sundays. And as far as the facilities are concerned, maybe we could work something out. We've agreed this isn't a great set-up long-term. But for now, let's see if we can make do. This kid has been moved around all over the place so many times it makes your head spin. He needs to settle somewhere for a while. Meantime, Pat here can try to find a foster home. I've known people who've taken in some pretty weird kids, even adopted them. So far, Flannelmouth has been great. Hasn't caused a bit of trouble."

Flannelmouth noticed he'd left out the part about running over to N-town.

Father Morrissey picked right up on the invitation. "Yes, father, you show me around. Meanwhile, I'm sure Ms. Spetrino has a lot to talk about with the young man."

They went off, chatting like old friends. Pat didn't seem so cheery.

"O.K., let me see," and she began looking at some notes in the notebook she always carried with her. "All right, I need to get some social history."

Why does she need to do that? he thought. They must have volumes on me already. Probably it's going to be like the long list of questions they ask every time at the medical clinic. Sometimes two or three people in a row asking the same questions.

The questions came and Flannelmouth reeled off the answers like a machine. Once or twice she was looking somewhere else and then tuned back in and had to ask him to repeat his answer.

They'd been at it for twenty minutes or so when the two padres came back to the office. Now they were Greg and Jack.

Father Morrissey said to Pat, "O.K., I think this can work."

She scowled, and he said, "Just for now, of course." Somehow that didn't please the lady.

"Tell you what, Pat. I think you and Greg should work out a plan for what needs to be changed. And see what the county or the state can do to help with the cost. The father here thinks he knows some people up in Wyman who would be willing to throw in a few bucks." Turning to Father Morgan, "I really like that idea of setting up a temporary shelter." Then to her, "You see, Pat, what he's thinking is, if he makes the necessary changes for Flannelmouth here, this could be for a shelter for homeless folks after the young man goes." Seemed very pleased with himself.

Pat shrugged and let out one of her little 'ugh's. "I'll have to run this all past my supervisor. So don't do anything yet, Father Morgan. I'll get back to you in the next couple of days."

It looked like a win win for everybody but Lady Pat. Flannelmouth had a new appreciation of Father Greg. No dummy. Done like a champion.

After the other two left, Flannelmouth asked, "So how did you do it?"

"In the first place, I didn't do it, you did."

"Me? I just...."

"No," said Father Greg, "I was figuring there was no way we could meet all their expectations. But when you asked Pat there to break it down, what exactly wasn't up to standards, it took her off guard. She breezed in here the first time, decided she didn't like it, and after that everything was no no no. I've seen the shrinks do that. First shrink makes a quick call in the first twenty seconds, writes it up; it gets passed along to the next, who goes looking for confirmation, and pretty soon everybody agrees the patient is A, crazy, or B, reacting to deprivation, or C, just bad bad bad."

"But the Father," he said. "How'd you bring him around."

"Oh, that." Father Greg smiled. "I knew about Father Morrissey some years ago. Let's say he had a little problem, which is why he got moved to the diocesan office. He knew that I knew and, well, we just decided there was no point in dwelling on the past."

"Oh." Flannelmouth decided he wouldn't dwell on the past either.

Chapter 4.

Mr. Rat.

Is there any creature on God's green earth more detestable than a rat? The question had often occurred to Flannelmouth over the years he had lived all too close to the demons. Along with the equally perplexing question of why God would even have created such a despicable being in the first place. Hadn't the Irish saints dispatched these villains with clever speech? Flannelmouth, one gifted with the art of speech, fancied literally talking one of the devils to death. What he didn't know was that he was about to have an opportunity to match wits with a rat.

Very early one Saturday morning -- Father Greg's one chance during the week to sleep in -- Flannelmouth, by nature an early riser, went into the kitchen to get himself some breakfast. And there in the middle of the kitchen table of all places sat a rat cleaning up some stray crumbs from the previous night's dinner. Oh, he was a handsome one, with sleek coat and ears of pink contrasting nicely with the gray of the fur. But such esthetic considerations were quickly trumped by the desire to get rid of the pest as soon as possible. The rat, sensing a certain lack of hospitality, made a rapid descent from the table and scurried into a crack between the refrigerator and the stove.

Flannelmouth washed off the table several times, then proceeded to open the refrigerator and prepare for breakfast. A quarter hour later, as he was finishing his raisin bran, Father Greg walked in.

"We have a visitor, father."

"Oh, this early?" Father Greg ducked his head back into the corridor and looked around, then returned. Flannelmouth shook his head and nodded toward the escape route.

"Mice?"

Flannelmouth shook his head a little more vigorously.

"You mean.... Shit!" A new addition to the father's vocabulary, or at least that part of it known to his young friend.

"Rat?"

"Rat indeed, father. Saw him with my own eyes."

"But the exterminators were here not a week ago."

"Rats are smart, father. They can outwit many an exterminator, which may be why the exterminators still got business to do."

"O.K., I'll run by the True Value and pick up some rat poison."

"Wouldn't advise that, father. Rats'll take a little taste to see if they get sick before they really go after the stuff. Or else they can crawl into the wall and die, and you never get rid of the smell."

The lad obviously knew a thing or two about rats. The father's eyes kept shifting over to the crack between the refrigerator and the stove, as if expecting to see the enemy show its face any minute,

"Then what do we do?"

"Traps is best, father."

"I hate those things. You could lose a finger. Nothing like mousetraps."

"Oh, I know, father. Have to be careful setting them up."

"All right, as soon as I've had some breakfast, I'll go buy a rat trap."

"I should go with you."

Father Greg didn't object.

Out on West 14th Street, the pair maneuvered around the gathering foot traffic. Father Greg led the way to the little storefront, one of a dying breed. Inside, an Asian woman on a raised platform surveyed the scene.

Father Greg went up to her. "Rat traps?"

"I don't know, try back corner there," motioning toward a stack of cartons that reached almost to the ceiling.

The two walked around the end of the stack and found themselves in a little area with shelves holding an odd assortment of household items. At one end of a bottom shelf were mousetraps, boxes with pictures of lightning spearing dead mice, and bug sprays of all sorts.

An Asian man came out of a narrow aisle. "What you want?"

"A rat trap," said Father Greg.

"Oh, nowadays use poison. Work much faster," and the man broke out in a big smile.

"No, we want a trap. You got traps?" He looked over at Flannelmouth, who nodded.

"Let's see. You wait here. I check," and he disappeared through a doorway in the back wall. In a few minutes he returned holding two rat traps. He held one out to Father Greg, who took it, looked it over, and nodded.

Flannelmouth reached past the father and grabbed the other trap out of the man's hand.

"Hey, this kid with you?"

"Yeah, he's with me."

Flannelmouth took the first trap from Father Greg and held them up beside each other. He gave the first trap back to the man. Holding the other trap away from him a little bit, he raised the steel bar on the spring a couple of inches and let it go. The bar smacked hard against the bed of the trap, causing him to drop it. He picked it up off the floor and said, "We'll take this one."

Father Greg was about to head toward the front of the store when Flannelmouth said, "Wait."

"What now?"

"Wire. We need strong wire and some nails." To the man, "Where's wire? You know, like 20 gauge. And nails."

"Wire on shelf right there," nodding up the aisle. "Nails same side only farther down."

The two went looking for the items while the man went off in the other direction.

"What was that all about?" asked the father, "What was wrong with the first trap, for instance?"

"It was bent a little, father. Probably already used. You gotta watch those people."

"Well, you and I are going to have a little talk about 'those people' some time. And why are we getting wire? Gonna string up that varmint, podner?"

"You got to anchor the trap. Otherwise the rat can drag it into his hole with him."

Visibly impressed, the father fell silent.

Later, back in the kitchen, the two went to work. Father Greg waited for instructions from the master. Flannelmouth assembled the purchases in the middle of the table. Without looking up, "Hammer?" Like a surgeon asking for a scalpel.

Father Greg went to the little back hall off the kitchen and returned in a minute with the desired implement. Flannelmouth flipped the trap upside down, stretched the wire over it near one end, and said, "We need a nail and the hammer, father."

Father Greg dutifully opened the box, took out a nail, and handed it and the hammer to the young man. Flannelmouth held the wire with one finger.

"Could you hold the wire just so, father?" The latter put his finger on the wire and hoped his companion was as skilled at driving in nails as he seemed to be at outwitting rats.

Flannelmouth placed the nail close to the wire and drove it in about halfway. Then he hammered it down over the wire until it pressed it into the wooden base. Bringing the end of the wire alongside the other strand, he repeated the process. Father Greg took another deep breath.

The lad next gave a tug on the wire and said, "O.K., step one. Now we have to put the other end of the wire around that water pipe down there next to the fridge."

They were down on their knees now, and Flannelmouth wrapped the wire several times around the pipe and brought the end around to make a knot. Again the tug on the wire and a nod of the head. They helped each other get back up.

"Now for the bait," said Flannelmouth.

"Cheese?" said his pupil.

"No, father, peanut butter -- and a few nuts to mix with it if there are any around." He wasn't about to waste perfectly good cheese on the scoundrel.

Father Greg took the peanut butter out of the fridge, placed it on the table, and went searching for nuts in the cupboards. Flannelmouth meanwhile fetched a small plate and a knife from the dish rack. The father was soon back with a package of pecan pieces. "Salted O.K.?"

"Perfect," said the other. He put a blob of peanut butter on the plate, then mushed in some of the nut pieces with his finger. Next he gave the taste test to the concoction and nodded with satisfaction.

"Now we put the bait on that little metal plate there...yes, that's it."

Down on the floor again with the nut mix, the father smeared a generous portion on the place indicated.

"Now we set the trap," said the youth, getting down beside Father Greg. He nodded to the father as if to say, "Want to give it a try?'

The other shook his head vigorously and laughed. For some reason it sent the two of them into a fit of giggling. It took them a while to settle down. Without a word, Flannelmouth pulled up the murderous steel bar and brought it all the way over to the other side, then positioned the hold bar over it, and slipped the hook in the end into the lock mechanism. Like a conductor about to begin a soft largo passage, he gradually raised his hands. The trap held. Then ever so gently he pushed the assemblage back toward the wall and pulled a box of Brillo pads over in front of it so it was out of sight.

"Bravo, we did it," shouted Father Greg. He shook Flannelmouth's hand.

"Now the rest is up to Mr. Rat," said Flannelmouth, letting out a long breath.

Several times that day, Father Greg suggested they go inspect the trap. No, said his mentor, we'll wait until morning.

Later, when the women came in to prepare for Sunday's service, the father told them excitedly what he and Flannelmouth had done. For some reason they seemed not to share his enthusiasm. And when the people arrived for the Seventh Day Adventist service, Father Greg suggested they had enough on their minds and shouldn't be bothered with any distractions.

Flannelmouth was up early as usual the next morning. He went immediately into the kitchen, where he beheld two tiny clawed feet jutting out from behind the Brillo box. A litle nod, then he went to work getting breakfast.

In a while, Father Greg came in wearing his gray-blue shirt with the clerical collar attached and navy blue trousers. He was all business when he was getting ready for the Sunday service. Flannelmouth nodded toward the Brillo box without saying a word.

"Oh, great, got him," said the father. "I was wondering if we should've got more traps. Maybe there are more in there."

"Not likely, father, with the exterminators coming every so often. He was probably a loner checking out the territory. If we left him alone, he might bring the family."

"Do you want to...uh...?"

"We can wait, father. He's not going anywhere. After church we can clean it up."

It was early afternoon before they got around to the cleanup. Flannelmouth pulled the Brillo box to one side. It had been a messy job with blood spattered around the site.

"Yuk," said the father. "I'll have Luis clean it up in the morning. But we should get rid of the body now. I'll get a couple of plastic bags."

Flannelmouth stood looking at Mr. Rat, lying serenely there, his spirit having departed for whatever place is reserved for his ilk in the netherworld.

"What's the problem?" asked Father Greg.

"My dad used to say we should respect the dead, no matter how bad they were in life."

"Oh, right," and the two of them stood silently gazing at the results of their handiwork.

As if speaking for the two of them, Father Greg said, "Proper burial," and Flannelmoth nodded gravely.

On a warm Sunday night in June, Mr. Rat was wrapped in a scarf a child had left behind at the church some years before and placed gently in a freshly dug hole in the back recesses of the church property. Flannelmouth sprinkled water from an empty coke bottle over the remains while Father Greg read from the Book of Common Prayer. The father then scooped dirt on top and tamped it down firmly, and Flannelmouth erected a wooden sign above saying 'Mr Rat may he rest in pease.'

Thus endeth the story of Mr. Rat.

Chapter 5.

Pamela.

It would be wrong to assume that Mr. Rat died in vain, for had he not helped with the bonding between the minister and his young charge? Indeed, the battle of wits with the evil one had brought our two friends together in a way that no human could have hoped to. Now, however, came along someone who would perhaps have the opposite effect.

Here is how it all began. One morning, as Flannelmouth finished his kitchen chores and headed for his toothbrush, there appeared in the corridor a woman of such rare beauty that it virtually took the young man's breath away. Flaxen was her hair, with eyes both round and wide.

"Hi. Greg here?" A voice like the tinkling of distant church bells.

"Uh.... He's up in his study, ma'am. Do you know the way? I can...."

"Sure, I know how to get there. Let's see, are you the new tenant? What is it they call you? Flannelmouth, right?"

The lad felt a flush in his face he'd never experienced. "Yes ma'am."

"Greg has told me lots about you. I'm Pamela. I assume he's told you about me."

"Uh, no ma'am."

Just then Father Greg came down the stairs. "Oh, hi, Pam. I see you've met Flannelmouth."

He came over, wrapped his arms around her and gave her a noisy kiss. Right on the mouth.

"Hey, Flannelmouth, meet the future Mrs. Morgan," said the father as she stood beaming at him. She waved a ring with a big boxy stone in the face of our friend, who stared in confusion.

"So all I know is 'Flannelmouth.' You have a back name?" She was looking straight at him with a lovely smile on her lovely face.

Totally unhinged, the youth managed, "Finnegan, ma'am."

"Finnegan? You're kidding. Oh, man. Greg, my love, I'm going to have to borrow your young friend next Saturday while you cook up your weekly sermon."

The father looked as puzzled as Flannelmouth was feeling.

"June 16th. Do you know what June 16 is?"

The father smiled and nodded. "Oh. Yeah, Bloomsday."

"Bloomsday indeed."

"Pam was an English major. Specialized in Joyce in graduate school."

"Joyce, father? Joyce who?"

"No, it's Who Joyce. James Joyce, to be exact."

Flannelmouth shrugged. "Never heard of the gentleman."

"Well," said the lady Pamela, "you're going to meet the gentleman Saturday at Lakeside Park, though he's been dead for almost three quarters of a century."

Mr. Rat still fresh in his mind, Flannelmouth felt a certain discomfort at that news.

"But first things first, Greg. Today we're looking up reception facilities, remember?"

"Oh, yeah, that's right. Look, hon, I have somebody coming in at ten. Can we just...?"

A look of irritation flashed across the lady's face and was gone. Looked like they'd been down this road before.

"How long will you be tied up? I'm supposed to have lunch with Vivian. I suppose I could delay it a little," and she took a cell phone out of her purse and flicked it open.

"This shouldn't take too long," said the father. "Housing is giving the woman a hard time. Two kids under three. She may be out on the street by the end of the month." His eyes were pleading.

"I'm sure she may," said Pam. Big uh-huh. "O.K., guess I should sit tight. I'll be up in the library. Let me know if its going to run past 11:30," and she turned, went to the stairwell, and was soon gone.

The father twisted his mouth to one side, then turned to Flannelmouth with a grin. "That's Pam. We're getting married in September. Her father's a priest up in Allendale."

Flannelmouth knew only that Allendale was a weathly suburb off somewere to the north of the city.

"Hey, that sounds neat," said Father Greg. "Going to Bloomsday, I mean. We'll get you in touch with your roots yet, old friend. Maybe even beats Jonathan Swift."

To Flannelmouth it was all English lit, Irish, whatever. It was still a murky and mysterious world where he was continually trying to catch up but always felt like he was getting further behind.

"Meanwhile, today is math day. Geometry. Remember, the formulas are all in the back. Just put a piece of paper in there so you don't have to keep looking for the page. You just have to figure out which formula to plug in."

'Just' was a very flexible word, the lad had found. In this case, it might mean spending the better part of an hour trying to figure which formula to use to solve a problem.

About then, there was a noise at the end of the corridor, and a heavy-set woman came into view leading a small toddler by each hand They were wiggling to get free, but she held them tightly.

"Oh, there's my appointment," said Father Greg. "Hi, Ms. Lopez. Here I come," and he left Flannelmouth to plumb the depths of geometry on his own.

He sat in the kitchen with the math book, a sheaf of papers, three pencils, and a calculator in front of him. But it didn't take long for his mind to drift up to the library and the ethereal being sitting up there.

The swan sweeps in across the dark pool and slides smoothly into the water with barely a ripple. It arches its graceful neck against the white feathers along its back and shakes a few drops of water off the tip of its bill. Ah, then this loveliest of creatures begins a magical transformation as it turns into the Princess Derbforgaill. Fair and yet more fair even, she awaits the mighty Cuchulainn, her lover. He comes to her, and together they glide down the river on a mighty barge redolent with the perfume of a thousand flowers to mysterious places yet unknown.

He thinks of the lovely Pamela alone upstairs in the library and imagines doing many wondrous and exciting things with her and feels an old stirring down below.

Legend has it that the Princess Derbforgaill married, not the mighty Cuchulainn, but his son.

And oh the many journeys the imagination of a healthy fourteen-year-old can travel. Wonderful, wonderful, most wonderful, wonderful, and yet again, wonderful.

Alas, reality has a way of disrupting our dreams at the worst possible time. "Flannelmouth." It was the father at the door. "Pam and I have some errands to do. I should be back by 12:30; (then to her) right, hon?"

She nodded and shrugged, then turned to the lad with her gorgeous smile. "Don't forget, Flannelmouth. Saturday. I'll pick you up at 9:30. O.K.?"

He nodded and waved as they left.

Oh yes, sweet Derbforgaill, I shall await thee.

Saturday morning was bright and unusually cool and breezy for the middle of June. With more than normal alacrity, Flannelmouth bolted down breakfast, jumped in and out of the shower, brushed teeth, and dressed. He wore his best T-shirt, the one with the picture of Malcolm X on the front.

The father was still just getting up when Pamela arrived. She was wearing a navy blue T-shirt with white letters RE:JOYCE across the front.

"Here," and she tossed a T-shirt to Flannelmouth, "uniform of the day. Go ahead, put it on."

He scampered to his room, quickly took off the Malcolm X shirt and put on RE:JOYCE in its place. Back in the kitchen, Father Greg was making a cup of coffee while Pamela stood studying the notes and bulletins on the refrigerator door.

"Hey, neat," said the father when he saw the shirt on Flannelmouth.

"Triple pun," said the lady. "It's about Joyce, of course; it's a time to rejoice; and it's a Joyce retrospective. One of Tom Pettit's creations."

It all went sailing over Flannelmouth's head.

At the mention of the name, the smile drained off the father's face. "Oh, is he back in town? I thought...."

"He was out on the coast for a while. You know Tom. Just a drifter at heart. Look, that was a long time ago. Besides, I understand he's up in New York trying out for a play. He won't even be at Bloomsday." She came over and gave Father Greg a hug and a long kiss and stage-whispered, "I love you."

The father patted her arm a couple of times.

"Anyway, said Pamela, "it's nice to know you can be jealous. That's like me with all those people you spend your time rescuing in the neighborhood," and she gave him a quick peck on the cheek.

Then she picked up her purse, grabbed Flannelmouth by the elbow, and headed for the door. "C'mon, friend, we've got to get you connected with your past."

"So tell me about Flannelmouth Finnegan. God, that name. You could probably have a great career in Hollywood." They were zipping along the interstate toward the lake. New territory for Flannelmouth.

"Oh, not much to tell, ma'am." Inside debate. Should he reel off the usual litany to the goddess? He wanted to impress her. Up this close he could smell some kind of perfume. She had a small scar on the right elbow, and her hand on the wheel was a little on the bony side.

"O.K., when did your people come from Ireland?"

"It was my father's people, ma'am. My mom was like Yankee or something. I never knew too much about that side of the family. "

"Oh?" Shift of tone. "Did your folks separate, or did you mom die when you were younger?"

"When I was three, ma'am. Died having my sister. She was adopted out, so we don't know what happened to her."

They were off the interstate now and seeing signs to Lakeside Park.

"Oh, that's awful. Greg lost his father when he was in high school. Dropped dead one day at work. His heart. The family had gone to the mother's folks' place for the weekend. Oh, and by the way, please drop the ma'am stuff. I'm Pam -- or Pamela if you like that better."

Ah, the lady Pamela. Flannelmouth's imagination was running in high gear . "I like Pamela myself, ma'am. Oh, excuse me. That just slipped out. Force of habit I guess."

"So do I. Pamela and Flannelmouth. Great combination."

Oh yes, fair lady, great indeed.

She put her credit card in the slot at the entrance to the park and waited for it to pop back out. "There. That takes care of the state parks and recreation department. Now let's see. We're looking for parking Lot C."

In a few minutes she maneuvered into a vacant spot in the row of cars. In the distance he could see the lake. There were people walking around in various stages of dress, from one old couple in sweaters to kids in swimsuits.

"Ah, there they are." They headed toward a knot of maybe 40 or 50 people at one end of a field overlooking the lake shore. Everybody was wearing the RE:JOYCE T-shirt.

"High, Jim, this is my friend Flannelmouth Finnegan. You bet, right out of the old country....Annette, meet a Finnegan. Yes, I know....Sally dear. Is Bob...? Oh, I'm sorry to hear it. Nothing serious I hope...."

The names went in one of Flannelmouth's ears and out the other without leaving a trace.

An old man with a white beard stood blocking their path. Pamela suddenly spotted him. "Dr. Parran!

My god, somebody said you were in the hospital." She ran up and threw her arms around him, then turned to our friend.

"Flannelmouth. Come meet my former lit professor."

The old man toddled over to where Flannelmouth stood rooted to the spot and extended his hand. There was a noticeable tremor in it. The boy shook it. It was weak to the grasp.

"Meet my friend Flannelmouth Finnegan, Dr. Parran," said Pamela, "I'm introducing him to a bit of his heritage."

"Finnegan is it? Well, young man, I hope you are awake this morning."

Pamela started smiling and nodding. "You haven't lost a bit of it, have you?"

Flannelmouth knew there was a joke in there somewhere, but he didn't get it. Oh well, these bookish folks have their ways, he thought

A little further along, Pamela stopped walking.

"Oh damn. What's he doing here?" She'd spotted a guy with a ponytail and a beard. He saw her and came over.

"Hi, Pam, how are things?" Sounded a little like somebody Flannelmouth had seen on TV. The guy came up close and gave Pamela a hug and a kiss on the cheek.

"Hi, Tom. Things are fine. This is my friend, Flannelmouth Finnegan." All in a kind of monotone. Pamela seemed to have lost her happy mood for the moment.

"Hi, Flannelmouth." Tom shook his hand. Strong and calloused hands, like those of a construction work.

"Hi." The youth nodded, and that was that. Pamela ready to move on.

"See you around," said Tom after them. Pamela said nothing.

Meanwhile, everybody seemed to be waiting for something to happen. A woman at the edge of the group shouted, "O.K., places, people, places. Time to tour Dublin."

Folks were taking out books. Some were looking for a place to sit down on the ground. Pamela pulled a book out of the big bag she was carrying.

"Pick your favorite passage," said the woman in charge. "If somebody gets there first, just go on to another. It's all good."

There was a pause while people thumbed through the pages. Flannelmouth looked over at Pamela with a quizzical expression. She shook her head. "No, you're here just to listen. Don't try to figure it out, just listen and enjoy the sounds."

As people started to read, Flannelmouth tried to enjoy. The words were beautiful, indeed. He wondered what they would sound like in the voice of an Irishman. His father, for instance. The man could talk as if he were singing. Meanwhile, Flannelmouth noticed that Tom had moved around so he was right opposite Pamela in the circle of people. She was looking everywhere but at the man.

It got around to Pamela's turn. Her voice was strong and confident as she began, eyes never leaving the page.

"By lorries along Sir Rogerson's Quay...."

The voice had a hypnotic quality to it. Flannelmouth closed his eyes and let the words drift over him. He didn't understand a lot of the words. He didn't have to. Just that sweet voice.

Pamela finished her passage and stood waiting for the next. As others took their turn, the mesmerizing grace of the words sent Flannelmouth drifting off in another direction.

The maiden is busy doing home chores while her sisters go off to church in all their finery. In comes the hen woman to dress her up in white, then up on a fine white horse she goes, the horse with golden bridle. Off to church she rides, and as she goes, dress and horse slowly turn to deepest black and the bridle to burnished silver. Ashamed, she flees the scene....

The fellow Tom was reading now. He kept raising his eyes from the page to zero in on Pamela.

"...first I gave him the bit of seedcake...."

Pamela was looking everywhere else. "I should have known. Why is he doing this?"

"...and I gave him all the pleasure I could...."

Pamela's eyes were closed now, and her head was weaving back and forth a bit.

"...and yes I said yes I will. Yes."

Tom slowly closed the book, and their eyes locked together for a few seconds, then Pamela turned away. Not a happy look on her face.

"O.K., said the lady in charge, "lunch break. Back at one o'clock."

Tom had disappeared into the crowd. Pamela picked up her big bag and said, "Let's find us a table. Over there by the lake. One with shade if we can."

They are soon sitting at a picnic table looking off toward the lake.

"Ham and swiss on rye O.K. with you? Help yourself to chips out of the bag there. That's Pepsi in the thermos."

"Yes, that's fine, Pamela." He poured some Pepsi into a paper cup and offered it to her. Then he poured himself the same.

"I'm not very imaginative when it comes to food, I'm afraid," she said between bites.

"Oh no, this is fine." Anything from the hands of this sweet lady.

Friend Tom came around the end of the table with a paper bag in his hand and prepared to sit down.

"Er, excuse me, Tom. I'm talking with my friend here," said Pamela. "Also, you're blocking our view of the lake."

He shrugged and walked off, the lady struggling meanwhile to get back on course.

"So tell me," turning to Flannelmouth with a slight shudder, "How do you like Bloomsday?"

"Oh it's fine, really. The man certainly knew how to write. My father was poetic. Never wrote anything, but he could tell wonderful stories. Could have been an Irish tenor."

"So what happened to him?"

"The good lord only knows. Probably kicking around a saloon somewhere." Flannelmouth hunched his shoulders for a moment.

"That's terrible. Do you miss him? Greg missed his father terribly."

"I suppose I do. He was a good man except for the drink. He'd beat me for nothing when he came back from one of his toots. Afterward he'd apologize and try to make things up to me. I hated that worse than the beatings. He was pitiful."

"So who took care of you?"

"Took care of myself pretty much I guess."

"Greg's a fine man," said Pamela. Flannelmouth was glad to get the attention off himself. He could only imagine what she was thinking of him now.

"He's so dedicated to his work. I think its the perfect preparation for his career."

"Career?"

"Yes. A few more years of this and then, you know, we'll find a church where we can, you know, settle down, raise a family, make a life for ourselves."

"Oh, I didn't...."

"My dad has connections. But of course Greg will have none of that. Dad tried to help him with his debts at the seminary, but he'd have none of that either. Stubborn to the core. But I guess that's what I really love about him."

Flannelmouth wanted to ask some questions but thought better of it and just nodded in agreement.

The afternoon was taken up with more readings. Flannelmouth tried to stay focused, but it was no use.

The lovely Derbforgaill and the mighty Cuchulainn keep floating by on their flower-bedecked barge, going to places as yet unknown.

The final slot was reserved for Dr. Parran. He had trouble keeping his place and had to be nudged back on course a few times. The old man got a standing ovation at the end.

On the way back to St. Luke's, Pamela said, "By the way, don't say anything about our running into Tom, O.K.? Greg gets a little upset, you know."

Flannelmouth thought he knew. His lips were sealed.

Late one Saturday afternoon, Flannelmouth and the father were out on 14th Street, visiting a sidewalk sale. People were bunched around some of the stalls, forcing our friends to go out into the street to get around them. The stalls had old clothes, books, and kitchenware mostly.

Flannelmouth stopped at a tray of books, wondering if he might see something by the celebrated Joyce. It was hard to tell one item from another. The boy's uncertain acquaintance with the written word didn't exactly help.

By chance his eye lit upon a book with "love" in its title, and with the discovery an inspiration began to form in our friend's brain. If he could but give the book to the lovely Pamela, his fantasy of wonderful things to come might come to pass. He was holding a collection of fliers thrust into his hand at a health clinic's table. With a skill borne of many such occasions, he briefly set the fliers down on the book, then picked them up and tucked them under his arm. Presto, the book had disappeared.

Back at his room later, he inspected his new acquisition. On the cover was a picture of some men and women and the words, *Love Speaks Its Name*. A quick look inside revealed that it was a collection of poems. Not troubling to try to decipher the contents, he closed the book quickly and tucked it into the drawer under his bed. Now the only problem was to find the appropriate occasion to present it to the lady of his dreams.

Chapter 6.

Settling in.

If there was one thing that characterized Flannelmouth Finnegan more than anything else, it was a lack of rootedness. What has been a major trauma for countless people of this world since time immemorial was for our friend just a part of the natural order. It lent itself to a certain ease of connecting with strangers, together with a shallowness which tended to rob relationships of real meaning.

Flannelmouth may in fact have been in the vanguard of a new normal in a world increasingly characterized by the arms-length intimacy of Facebook, easy mobility, and generations within families separated by thousands of miles.

Now, for the first time maybe, that yearning for a sense of home that lies within each of us stirred in our young friend. In subtle ways, not apparent even to him, he began to make the world of St. Luke's his own. It was most manifest in the weekly routines he gradually became a part of. Those associated with the food cupboard, for example.

Each Thursday, Frank, a volunteer from a suburban church, came by in his pickup to take Father Greg and Flannelmouth to the area food bank to get groceries for Friday's food cupboard. Frank's friend Amos followed in his station wagon.

Flannelmouth liked to ride in the back of the pickup with the wind streaming through his hair and the metal truck floor banging up against his rear end.

Sometimes Frank would tap the brakes to make Flannelmouth pitch up toward the front. Neat guy that Frank. Amos was older. Not much of a sense of humor. He always looked as if he was in a hurry to get off to some place else.

The food bank was in a long-closed factory turned warehouse, a few blocks from the river. The truck and the station wagon swung into spaces in a row of parked vehicles to the side of the building. Father Greg hopped down and went inside. He emerged in a few minutes with an order sheet. "O.K., we're fourth in line," and he climbed back up into the truck cab.

A forklift emerged through a gaping doorway in the side of the building, deposited a stack of packing cases and went back for more. Flannelmouth thought it would be great to drive one of those things. The driver obviously knew what he was doing. Father Greg said he'd got laid off at the main terminal on the lake two years before and never called back. There was a lot of that along the riverfront. Frank said it was because of all the jobs shipped overseas. Wasn't like that in his day.

A second man was in charge of the stacks of cases. He finally signaled to Frank, and the truck crept forward. Everybody knew his job. The father pointed at which cartons to bring while he marked the order sheet. Frank and Avery began lugging the cases over and dumping them into the back of the truck. Flannelmouth's job was to push them around to make room for more. Stacking them was harder.

"Want some help up there?" asked Father Greg.

"No." Didn't sound entirely convincing, but Flannelmouth was determined to handle the job by himself. After a while he put up a hand, his chest heaving. The father waved the other two back, then nodded toward the station wagon. They started loading that while Flannelmouth caught his breath. Father Greg looked up, and Flannelmouth nodded. "O.K.," he yelled.

In another fifteen minutes they were done and headed back to St. Luke's. At the rear of the church they reversed the process. The men loaded the cases onto two battered hand trucks. Flannelmouth and the pastor pushed the trucks over to the outside entrance to the storeroom, where the three men moved the food inside and stacked it.

The final step was handshakes all around. "Good job, kid," said Frank. Amos nodded. Then the father invited them into the kitchen for a cup of coffee. Flannelmouth didn't care much for the taste, but with lots of milk and sugar it was O.K. Besides, he just liked being one of the guys.

Early Thursday evening the other volunteers came in to set up the food for the next day. They were an odd collection. Two old women plus the husband of one of them, a younger lady who said she was on the advisory board or committee or something, along with a few college students.

The board lady was in charge. She ran the whole thing like a military operation, though the others knew the routine well enough just to go about their duties on their own. They used the hand trucks to cart the stuff out of the storeroom and set it up on the long tables in the big room on the corridor.

Flannelmouth joined in, and he was soon something of a pet with the group. His job was to set up things on the tables, along with Marion, one of the college student regulars. Cereal went here, pancake mix there, canned goods after that, and so on. He got to where he could instruct any new volunteers where to put things.

Friday was food cupboard day. For two hours, people from the neighborhood walked in, picked up a paper bag from the stack donated by a local supermarket, and walked along the tables, picking up groceries as they went. Only one of everything to a customer.

The selection was limited, typically one brand of breakfast cereal, for example, but it was all of reasonable quality. There was a lot missing from the choices -- mainly perishables. The place lacked the refrigeration to make it feasible.

One mother asked for diapers. They tried that for a while, but demand was too irregular. It was a case of feast or famine. Feast meant taking up a lot of space needed for other items; famine produced resentment from some of the customers.

Same thing with toilet paper. When some neighborhood kids got hold of a few of the rolls and threw them around to see the paper streamers fly by, that one was abandoned in a hurry.

Father Greg made sure the folks were greeted with a smile. Treat them like customers, he said, very important customers, because in God's eyes that's what they were. One college student who continued to make snide comments about the customers was asked not to come back.

It took Flannelmouth, well familiar with the baser instincts in his fellow human beings, a while to get used to this new way of thinking. Even then, he wasn't totally convinced, but he kept his doubts to himself.

Occasionally there would be rumors that people were selling what they got at St. Luke's for drug money. If a volunteer brought that up at one of the monthly meetings, Father Greg would shrug and say he had no idea. He made clear his priority was feeding the hungry, not policing the behavior of the customers. Above all, he talked about the young children who trotted after their parents or would start running up and down the corridor while their parents picked up food.

At one of the sessions, a young volunteer suggested that the people getting the food should put in some work in exchange. When Father Greg turned aside the suggestion, the volunteer persisted. Wouldn't people feel better about themselves if they were doing something in return? They might even gain some work skills in the bargain. Father Greg ended that session rather abruptly. The proposal made eminently good sense to Flannelmouth, who asked about the exchange afterward. He quickly realized that he'd crossed a line of some kind and dropped the subject.

"Hello, Ms. Ramos, and how is that fine son of yours today?" Flannelmouth was gradually getting to know names.

"Yes, well we had those last week, Tina, but we're all out for now. Maybe next time around."

"Just one, Denny. Aha, I know, sir. That's not much to fill the belly, is it?"

Around ten-thirty, the father would come down from his office and check things out.

"Can't we get a different kind of iced tea, father?" Mrs. Snyder, the woman in charge, always had something to complain about. "That stuff is so sweet. I'm sure it's not doing some of those men a lot of good."

"I'll check with the food bank. We're kind of at their mercy, you know."

Flannelmouth wondered if the father ever followed through, or even whether Mrs. Snyder really expected him to. Each week it was another item or two. Just one more part of the routine, he decided.

There were times when Father Greg took on a different role: taking a customer out into the corridor to talk about a personal crisis the person was having at the time. Occasionally he would take the person up to his office for a more extended consultation and phone calls to agencies that might help.

And then there was Luis. With the decline in St. Luke's resources, the custodian's hours had been cut in half. Now he came in just five mornings a week. That meant he wasn't around to let people in in the afternoon. He was the one person Flannelmouth had trouble connecting with at first.

"Has Luis got a problem with me?" he asked Father Greg during dinner one night.

"Not that I know. Why do you ask?"

"He seems very unfriendly. I say something to him and all I get is a nod and a grunt."

"Could be the language. Or the fact that Luis is mad at the world. That's just his way, I guess." Ready to move on to other matters.

Flannelmouth wasn't ready to move on. "Maybe he resents me being here."

The father sat for a couple minutes. "The only thing I can think of is that you came along about the time we had to cut his hours. Never said anything, but it had to be a big setback for him. He has a wife and two kids. I tried everything I could think of to avoid it."

"So it's like I *am* the cause. You supporting me and all means you can't pay him as much."

"No. County is paying us for your upkeep. Food basically. Doesn't cost St. Luke's a penny."

"Oh." Pause, then, "I'd still like to get over the hump with the man."

"I can say something to him."

"No, father, I have to do it."

He resolved to take it on as a special task. From then on he made it a point to push past the nods and grunts.

"You got kids I hear," he said one day when he found Luis polishing the lecterns up in the sanctuary.

"Yeah, two." Little glimmer of a smile.

"Hey, neat. How old are they?"

Luis put down the cloth and reached into his hip pocket. He pulled out a worn leather wallet and opened it to reveal a photo of a woman and two young boys.

"Dat was a few years ago. Dat's Andy on the left. He's fourteen now. Doin' O.K. in school. Dat's Angel. He's nine. School, well....," and he gave a shrug.

"Know how old I am?"

"Dunno, sixteen, maybe seventeen."

Flannelmouth shook his head. "Fourteen, same as Andy."

"No kiddin'! Ain't that sump'n." Big smile -- the first one Flannelmouth could remember.

"You got Angel in the after-school here?"

"Nah, you know kids got their own routine."

"They could help him with homework. They do that kind of thing."

Luis shrugged and went back to his polishing. After that he always gave Flannelmouth a big smile when they ran into each other. And when the after-school program started up again in the fall, it would have a new member named Angel Ortega.

One of the routines Flannelmouth both hated and looked forward to each week was schoolwork.

"Father, there's no school now. Why do I have to do schoolwork in the middle of the summer?"

"Because you have a lot of catching up to do. You'll be starting regular school in September. We can't have you way behind everybody else now, can we?" A question not necessarily looking for an answer.

Tuesday and Friday were the days Jim Landry came by in the afternoon to work with Flannelmouth on reading and math. ("It's 'Jim,' not 'sir' or 'Mr. Landry.' O.K.?" It was totally O.K. with Flannelmouth.) He got so he looked forward to the ex-high school teacher's visits. And the guy was colored, too.

"Now Flannelmouth -- man, do I like that name -- remember what we said about old Pythagoras? You been adding them first. Square them first, then add...

Come on, that's what the calculator's for.... Right, right... O.K., high five, man."

It was painfully slow, but Flannelmouth felt he was beginning to get it. Math, that mysterious world he had never been able to penetrate. Sometimes Jim would make a face as if to say "idiot!" But you knew underneath he was with you.

If things got too bogged down, Jim would suggest they go out and shoot a few baskets in the parking lot. This was no Father Greg. Flannelmouth had met his match and then some. It was only later that he learned that Jim had coached two teams at Central High to the state semi-finals. But, win or lose, Flannelmouth loved it. Significantly, the father didn't have to prod him to do his homework. He wanted Jim to see he was learning.

"How were your grades in school?" Father Greg asked one night at dinner.

"Oh, not so good, father. I got bounced around a lot, you know. Just passed mostly."

"Jim thinks you got a brain in that head of yours."

It made Flannelmouth's day. Ever after that, he made sure his homework was all done and ready when Tuesday and Friday afternoons rolled around. One time when Father Greg invited him to go over to the park, he said, "Sorry, I got a little of my math to finish up."

Tuesday and Wednesday were the days Father Greg generally set aside to take care of everything else, from fighting to get the diocese to free up a little more money for St. Luke's, to taking a tenant to the housing office to keep from losing her apartment, to helping a distraught mother locate her son or daughter. He often took Flannelmouth with him. "Just a little basic education," he said.

On a particular Wednesday in July, he took Flannelmouth along when he went to the diocesan office. The issue had nothing to do with the fate of St. Luke's or anguishing parents or struggling tenants but the bishop's adamant stand against same-sex unions.

Father Greg was one of several priests to sign a petition calling for a different stand, and, as so often happened, he was the one expected to carry the flag into battle. His own congregation had no problem with his position on the issue. It was a different story with many churches in the diocese. Besides, he relished a little mix-up with what he considered a very oppressive hierarchy. He had suggested a small delegation would be better than a single person, but one by one the other priests announced unavoidable obligations that would keep them from the meeting. 'Subsequent engagements' was what Father Greg called them.

The father sat shuffling through some papers while they waited in the austere lounge with the garnet colored drapes and furniture to match. Flannelmouth stood at the long mahogany table in the center and moved the little stacks of brochures around like chess pieces.

"The bishop will see you now, father." The secretary gestured for him to go in.

Flannelmouth started to follow, but the secretary looked at the father, and he shook his head. "Wait here."

The lad sank into a big easy chair and dozed off.

He's at a wake, coffin in the middle, and everybody drinking like it's their last chance. His dad is there having a grand old time. Somebody shoves a fiddle in his hands and says play. He saya I don't know how but they say play and he's suddenly playing beautiful music. Star of the show he is.

Flannelmouth heard voices coming from behind the bishop's door. Angry voices that grew in volume. He couldn't make out what they were saying. Silence, then more talk at a lower volume. The door opened, and Father Greg walked out saying, "Come on, let's get out of here."

Flannelmouth followed him out, down the stairs, and out the front door. All the way home the father was fuming to himself. "And him talking about love between a man and a woman. He's a great one to talk, with his own brother knocking up the deacon's wife and covering it all up that way.

"Oh, excuse me, Flannelmouth. Talking to myself. Well, what the heck, it's part of your education."

The boy was sure it was, though he wasn't clear exactly what lesson he was supposed to take away with him.

The highlight of the week was none of these routines, but rather Monday. That was Father Greg's official day off. The diocese had been a strong supporter of the idea. In fact, they had insisted on it when the father's service to God and humankind appeared to be getting to be a 24/7 kind of thing.

Why the highlight? Because more than likely it involved Pamela. She often came Sunday afternoon and stayed over. Just as often, she stayed Monday night and left first thing Tuesday. As a substitute teacher in the schools, she always had the option of turning down an assignment, so was free to spend time in town when she wished. Living with her folks, she didn't really need the income.

Whenever Father Greg and Pamela were going some place on a Monday toot, they invited Flannelmouth along. They made quite a threesome as they played in parks, visited exhibitions, or stopped off at a restaurant for a meal. More than once, a stranger said 'your mom' while nodding in Pamela's direction.

No matter where they had been that day, it felt good to get back to the church, scare up some tomato soup and a grilled cheese sandwich, and maybe sit playing cards or dominos or just sitting. It touched off nostalgia in the two adults, but for Flannelmouth it was a taste of a wonderful world he had never known.

Flannelmouth was still infatuated with Pamela but had come to terms with the fact that Father Greg had first place in her heart. By now the book of love poems was a distant memory.

One Sunday afternoon, as the father lay snoring lightly on the couch in his office, Pamela whispered to Flannelmouth, "Tomorrow's Greg's birthday."

"Oh, I didn't know,"

She opened a paper bag and pulled out a book and a couple of gift cards.

"I should have got him something," said Flannelmouth.

"That's O.K., this can be from the both of us." She gave him the card with the green envelope and took the one with the rose-colored envelope for herself. Opening the card up and scribbling something on the inside, she handed the pen to Flannelmouth. "Here, she said."

He opened the card, thought for a moment, then wrote, 'Happy birthday to a good man the best,' in his awkward scrawl and signed it below: 'FF.'

"We'll take him to a restaurant tomorrow," she said.

"O.K. Or I could make the two of you breakfast in the morning," said Flannelmouth.

"Great. We need anything?"

"No, we got eggs and bagels in there. That ought to do it."

About that time, the father stirred and opened his eyes. It took him a minute to register. "Oh, I was asleep."

"That was obvious, dear," said Pamela, kissing him.

The father noticed them exchanging little smily glances, guessed that something was in the wind, but thought better of saying anything.

The next morning Flannelmouth dressed and went straight to the kitchen. He set to work with a purpose. The seven months he'd once spent in the home of a cooking expert -- one of his many temporary 'homes' over the years -- now came in handy.

Setting three places at the table, he next took a platter from the top shelf of the cupboard and placed it on the counter next to the stove. Let's see, bagels. Out of the fridge with them. They were soon sliced in half with the carving knife. Into the oven like so. Oh yes, butter and jam to the table we go. All right, six eggs out of the fridge -- and the milk of course. Salt -- salt, oh yeah, just borrow the shaker from the table.

Pamela poked her head in the door. She was holding the book and the birthday cards. "He's sleeping like a baby. Got to figure out something with the snoring, though. Oh, good, you're....you O.K. with that?"

"Yes, Pamela. Things are in good hands," said the expert.

She put the book and the cards in the middle of the table. "Anything I can do? You seem to have everything...."

"You could do coffee."

"Coffee, let's see, coffee...."

Hmm, thought Flannelmouth, those two are going to be off to a great start.

"Here, Pamela, check the fridge. Big jar of instant on the upper left hand shelf. We do fine with instant around here. There's a plastic measuring spoon inside. Put a heaping spoonful in each cup over there."

She put the bag of coffee on the counter, dug around inside, and held up the brown plastic scoop. "Step one," she said.

"Yes, Pamela, step one. Now put a heaping spoonful in each cup.... O.K., need a little more. Tell you what, put that back in the bag.... That's right. Now fill the scoop and level it off with your finger.... Good. O.K., you're doing fine. Now do the same with a second scoop, good, and, yes, pop it in the same cup."

"That's too much, Flannelmouth."

"No it isn't. You'll see. We like our coffee strong around here. Good. Do that with each cup.... Great. Now fill the teakettle about half with water and set it to boiling."

She did as she was told, until she got to the part about boiling the water. The teakettle was sitting on the largest of the four burners.

"No, slide the kettle over to the burner on the right. I'm going to be doing the eggs on the other one.... Good, now the button on the front of the stove.... The one just to the right of that.... Yes. turn it all the way to the right.... No, that's O.K. It'll pop on in a.... There, see? Flame's up under the kettle just fine."

He wondered what this advanced scholar of James Joyce had been doing during her college years. Getting waited on hand and foot, he decided.

The lesson over, he went back to what he was doing while Pamela slid into one of the chairs at the table, looking exhausted. She watched in fascination as the master went back to work.

"How did you learn this stuff?"

"Oh, I lived with a lady who wrote for the food page in the newspaper. The county put me there. She taught me lots.... You wouldn't believe all that goes into making an omelet.... Oh, would you mind fetching me the jar of dill in the last cupboard over there? Yes, bottom shelf.... Should be to the left of that one...got it."

A look of triumph spread across the lady's face as she put the jar down in front of Flannelmouth.

O.K., oh, the cheese. Thought there was some shredded back on the lower left-hand shelf.... Yes, good. Mixing bowl somewhere here. O.K., break eggs into the bowl like so. A little salt and a little dill. A little more dill. O.K., and we whip the eggs up and now the milk. And there we have it. Good.

"And now you cook them?" asked the audience.

"Oh no. We don't cook them till we're ready to eat them. Any stirrings from down the hall?"

"I'll go see," and she tiptoed out. She was soon back. "Not a peep." She sat down. "Oh, Flannelmouth, I'm never going to learn all this stuff." Looking like she was about to cry.

"But you're an educated lady. You'll learn." The expert sat down at the other end of the table. "Coffee? You could have some while we wait. I hear some stirrings in the kettle."

"That's all right, I'll wait." She was staring at the floor, a somber expression on her face.

"There's some good cooking lessons on TV if you got cable. And they have tons of cookbooks out there."

"I don't know, I guess you have to want to learn. I don't know...."

Just then they heard Father Greg coming. As he rounded the edge of the door jamb, "Hi, what's going on here? Oh, God, look at that."

"Happy birthday, darling."

"Happy birthday, father."

There were vigorous hugs all around.

"Now you two go sit at the table," said the chef. "Oh, Pamela, you can pour the coffee. Right, turn up the fire under the teakettle till it gets boiling again."

As she finished pouring the water into the cups, he turned back to the stove.

O.K., up with the broiler. And up with the burner. Oh, fat for the skillet. A quick trip to the fridge. Bottle of oil, O.K. The cooking lady liked butter, but the father said it was too much cholesterol. Into the pan. Check the broiler. O.K., bagels getting a faint hint of a tan. Into the pan with the egg mix. Tilt the pan so and tilt the pan so and tilt the pan so and O.K., cheese on top like so and bagels out of the oven and onto the counter next to the platter, and now we turn off the burner and the oven and up with the skillet -- heavy bugger -- and under the eggs with the spatula and roll her over into the platter like so and a sprinkle of a little of the dill on top like so and.... Perfect.

He arranged the bagels around the omelet, picked up his creation and presented it to his audience with a little bow. The audience went wild.

"Bravo, Flannelmouth, That's beautiful," said Father Greg. Pamela put her napkin up over her face and her head was shaking.

It was a beautiful start to what promised to be a beautiful day. Later that day, a birthday card was tacked up on the wall above the father's desk, and there it stayed. On it was an awkward scrawl reading

Happy birthday to a good man the best
FF

Chapter 7.

In search of roots.

Bloomsday had touched off in Flannelmouth a deep yearning he had been able to stuff way back into his unconscious these many years. His memory of his mother consisted of a few brief glimpses of events long past, fleeting, disconnected, and more than likely assisted by two albums of yellowing snapshots and stories from his father.

But his memories of his father were vivid, an odd mix of funny faces and Irish airs and the endless stream of songs and stories from the old country. Like most of his past associations, the images of his father had sunk into yesterdays, supplanted by new places and people. Most of the time he simply ignored the past and moved on with the times. Now the memories of his father came flooding back to disturb his sleep, along with the dreams born of the rich culture that never left him.

"Father" he said one summer evening as they walked the city streets in the fading light. "I've been thinking about what Pamela said that day we went to Lakeside Park."

"What's that, son?"

"I told her about my dad, and she said I must miss him and that you missed your dad a lot."

"Oh I still do. We had wonderful times together. Baseball was his sport. Followed just about every big league baseball team every season. I even got to go to a few games. He could rattle off the statistics like a sportscaster.

"He died all of a sudden, she may have told you. I was right in the middle of being a terrible teenager at the time. There was a while there after he died they didn't know what to do with me. Suspended from school, drinking, tried smoking pot for a while. My grades got so bad it didn't look like I'd ever make it to college. The dyslexia didn't help, of course. Finally got accepted at community college so I could bring my grades up."

Flannelmouth had a little trouble reconciling this picture with the uptight pastor next to him.

"It started me thinking, father, like maybe I should find out what's become of my dad."

"Sounds like a good idea. Any thoughts about where you might look?"

"There's some guys used to hang out with him. You could generally find them around the docks along the river, you know, near where it empties into the lake. I also know a few taverns that he used to go to pretty regular. They might know."

"Let's give it a try." The father put an arm around the boy's shoulder as they headed for home.

They were an odd pair, the priest and the teenager, as they entered Murphy's Golden Pub. A solitary old man sat at the bar jiggling a glass and staring at the Bulls and the Sixers going at it on the screen above. A lady was wiping the faux mahogany surface with a sponge and following with a dishtowel.

"Can I help you, father?" The lady had stopped her wiping. Father Greg let Flannelmouth do the talking.

"Have you seen Seamus Finnegan around, ma'am?"

"That old buzzard? I thought he was dead by now. We haven't seen him since Larry ran out of patience and booted him out of here, and him with an unpaid bill a mile long."

"He's the boy's father," said Father Greg, nodding in Flannelmouth's direction.

"Oh, sorry, father." Like she'd accidentally bumped into him while walking by.

The old man at the bar spoke up. "My god, you Seamus's boy? He used to bring you in as a tot and set you up on the bar there. Proudest poppa you ever saw."

"I remember," said Flannelmouth, "He'd start singing 'My Wild Irish Rose' and make me sing along with him. That was his favorite song. My mom's name was Rose."

"Do you know where we might find him?" asked Father Greg.

"You could check at the mission over on 7th Street," and the man downed the last of the contents of the glass and shoved it over toward the lady. "Sister Patrice Ann over there used to keep pretty good track of Seamus. If anybody knows his whereabouts, she would."

"I know where it is," said the Flannelmouth. It was clear the father didn't. Twenty blocks from St. Luke's and it could have been a couple hundred miles.

84

"Thanks," said Father Greg, as they took their leave. The old man raised the new glass that had been placed in front of him. "Bless you, boy, and blessings on you, too, father."

The lady was busy wiping off the bar.

The house on East 7th, crammed into a row of identical structures that lined the sidewalk, had once been somebody's home. A sign announcing 'Sisters of St. Francis' was tacked onto one of the posts that lined the porch. The place had seen better days. Part of the screen on the wide bay window hung ripped and useless.

Father Greg, with Flannelmouth right behind, tried the door. It opened, revealing a long hallway with several rooms on the left.

"Hello?" No answer, but it sounded like someone talking in the last room. They went back and found a nun, maybe in her early forties, sitting in front of a computer and talking on the phone. She looked up, smiled, pointed to the phone, and nodded toward a sofa on the other side of the room. They went and sat.

"Yes, well anything you can.... Oh I know, the people have been wonderful.... Yes, we certainly apprec...yes, well thank you so much. Bye," and the phone went down on the cradle. She shook her head, still smiling and put up her hands.

"Sounds like St. Luke's," said Father Greg. "Keeps getting tougher out there, doesn't it?"

"St. Luke's, father? I don't believe I'm...."

"Over near West 14th. Episcopal."

"Oh," laughing, "I see, well yes, and you're right about the money. Everybody's hurting these days it seems. If it wasn't for the young men from the seminary helping out, I don't know what we'd do." She came over and sat in a chair across a battered coffee table in front of the sofa. "I thought the Episcopal Church...."

"Everybody thinks that, sister, which is part of the problem. St. Luke's is a very small church with a very big agenda. We're not necessarily favorites with the diocese, either."

A big nod from the sister. "Downtown has been trying to close us down for years." A little pause, then, "Well," rubbing her hands together, "what brings you two here this fine morning?"

"I should introduce us. I'm Father Morgan, St. Luke's parish, and this is my young friend, Flannelmouth Finnegan."

The sister jumped a little and blinked at the name, then laughed. "Well, yes, unusual name that. I'm sure there's a story behind it."

Flannelmouth got ready to go through the usual litany, but she went on, "By the way, I'm Sister Jennifer. So how can I help you?"

"It's the lad's father, Seamus Finnegan. The boy has lost touch with him and thinks you may be able to help. Somebody thought Sister Patrice Ann might know."

"Let me get the sister," and she hopped up and went out.

The two looked at each other. The father shrugged, "Worth a try."

In a few minutes Sister Jennifer returned, followed by an older nun. Father Greg got up, and

Flannelmouth took the cue. Sister Jennifer went over to get the desk chair.

"Here, let me...," said the father, but she waved him off and rolled the chair over to where the older woman was easing herself into the other chair.

"Sister Patrice Ann," raising her voice a few decibels," this is Father...Morton is it?"

"...Morgan..."

"Yes, Father Morgan. And this is, hmm, Mr. Finnegan."

"Yes," said Sister Patrice Ann, "Sister Jennifer said you were looking for the boy's father."

"That's right, we're hoping...."

"Finnegan. Tell me the name."

Flannelmouth spoke up. "It's Seamus, sister, Seamus Finnegan."

Sister Patrice Ann closed her eyes, nodded once, and slowly exhaled. The eyes stayed closed.

"Ah yes. I know the man well." Then, eyes opened and, looking straight at Flannelmouth, "So you're the son." There was a slight nod and a trace of a smile.

"Then you know where we can find him?" asked the father.

"Of that I'm not sure. Used to hang out at Murphy's pub a lot"

"We were just there. That's how we got to you."

"Oh, I see. Seamus usually finds his way here when things get particularly bad, but we never know when to expect him."

Sister Jennifer chimed in. "Somebody saw him down in that little patch under the bridge. Not too long ago, I think."

"You mean the Village?" said Father Greg.

"The Village indeed," said Sister Patrice Ann. "Not a nice place. There are knifings just about every night." She clearly knew the area. "You could try there...daytime, I suggest. The other place is the docks. He was a longshoreman before he hit the skids. He keeps in touch with his old buddies there."

Everybody just sat after that. Looked like Sister Patrice Ann had run out of ideas. Father Greg got up. "Well thank you anyway, sisters."

They said their goodbyes, and the father and Flannelmouth were soon back out on the sidewalk.

The Village, as it is called locally, is known far and wide. It even showed up in a PBS documentary on poverty and crime some years ago. Tucked up against the huge bridge abutment, invisible to the interstate traffic that roars overhead day and night, it is home to a vast and shifting population of ex-cons, drifters, and other lost souls. Often the final destination of society's rejects, it spawns violence and a kind of viciousness that feeds on itself. The police make frequent forays into the Village, never one cruiser alone, and then just as quickly they leave. For the most part, the city ignores the squalor and goes on about its business. What are often missed are the countless little acts of kindness among the inhabitants that make the Village minimally tolerable.

Neither Flannelmouth nor the father had ever ventured near the Village, and they approached it warily. Father Greg hoped the collar might afford him some protection. What they found was an assortment of men sleeping on the ground or on piles of trash they had managed to assemble into makeshift beds. A heavy odor of decay and urine lay over the place.

An old woman was walking around with a plastic trash bag, looking for who knew what? Flannelmouth approached her.

"Morning, ma'am, we're looking for Seamus Finnegan. You know him?"

The woman, unseeing, let go a stream of profanity and continued on her rounds. The two kept going. A man was sitting hunched up by a pile of bottles. He nodded as Flannelmouth went up to him and repeated the question.

"I hear he went to the hospital. Sick or something."

"And how long ago might that have been, sir?"

The man shrugged, and they moved on. No telling whether Seamus was dead or alive at this point.

"Hey." It came from a man coming up behind them at a trot. Flannelmouth and the father both tensed up. When the man came closer he said, "I hear you're looking for Seamus."

"Yessir, do you know where he might be?" said Flannelmouth.

"He's the boy's dad," said Father Greg.

"He's in the county hospital. Liver problem. That and diabetes, I think."

"Say, thanks" said the father. Then to Flannelmouth, "O.K., on to the hospital?" and the lad nodded.

As they climbed back into the father's ancient Honda, Flannelmouth said, "Not sure this is such a good idea, father."

"Why not?"

"Not sure what we're going to find when we get there. He was a lively sort when I knew him. Now...." and he raised his shoulders a bit.

"I think it's good to try to see him. It will mean a lot to him. And I think it will mean a lot to you, too." The father was thinking about his own father, wondering what it would have been like if he had lived.

"I sometimes think what my dad must look like now," said the boy. "He'd be older, of course."

"How old is he now?"

"I think in his late forties, maybe fifties, not quite sure."

The two lapsed into silence after that. They had left the more built up part of town and were on a four-lane main road with apartment buildings and a few large single dwellings interspersed with strip malls on either side. Up ahead was a hospital sign. A few more minutes, and they turned in at the hospital entrance and drove past a cluster of brick buildings to the left. The main hospital building rose several stories above its neighbors.

"This place has really grown. I can remember when it was just the main building." This comment by Father Greg, more of a space filler than anything else, drew no response from his young companion, whose mind was on other things. They swung around into the parking lot at the rear of the building. Bus 57 was just depositing its passengers at the main entrance. A couple of women in nurses' uniforms were waiting to board. One said, "Good morning, father," and nodded her head slightly.

"You know the lady?" asked Flannelmouth, who was beginning to think the man must be world famous.

"No, it's just the collar," the other laughed.

Inside, Father Greg led the way to the information desk at the rear of the lobby. Two women sat behind the desk, one busy knitting and the other half dozing over a magazine.

"Seamus Finnegan?" asked the father. That brought the woman with the magazine up with a start. Studying the computer in front of her, "How do you spell that first name?"

"Seamus, S-E-A...."

"Oh, oh, O.K. D Wing," she said. "D-2112. Take the elevator over there to the third floor and go to the left, through the double doors and all the way back. It's on the right." As they started to go, "Here, you'll need these," and she handed the father two adhesive 'visitor' labels.

D Wing consisted of two wide corridors lined with gurneys and wheelchairs, with doorways to patients' rooms and an endless flow of people in a variety of uniforms pushing carts, carrying trays of bottles, and conferring with each other. Halfway up was the nursing station with people working at computers, writing in ledgers, or laughing hysterically about something. Nobody paid any attention to the two visitors.

Father Greg said, "Over there. See, Room 2106. Just a few doors up."

Flannelmouth paused in front of the half-open door. Father Greg put an arm around him and led him inside. A curtain was drawn around the near bed, and somebody was talking in a loud voice. "That's right. We're taking you down for some tests, Mr. Cannon. O.K.?" You couldn't tell whether Mr. Cannon's feeble reply was a yes or a no.

Moving past the drawn curtain, Flannelmouth beheld his father asleep in the bed by the window. A mere shadow of the man he had known. Hair wispier and grayer than the lad remembered. There was a gray stubble on his chin, But what struck Flannelmouth most forcefully was the array of tubes that disappeared under the bedclothes here and there. Above and to the right, wiggly lines in different colors kept moving across the monitor screen, and the numbers next to them kept changing.

Father Greg came up behind Flannelmouth. "Oh, he's sleeping."

"We shouldn't disturb him," said the boy, who seemed ready to flee.

"Let's wait a bit. You stay here. I'll check at the nursing station," and he went out, leaving Flannelmouth alone with his dad.

He stared at his father, then gazed off where trees were rustling in the breeze and life went on like normal. In a few minutes, Father Greg returned with a stout black woman in an aide's uniform close behind.

"This is his son" said the father. Then to Flannelmouth, "This is Tamara. She's been tending your dad." The boy nodded.

"Oh yes, Mr. Finnegan is a fine man," said Tamara. "He was telling me stories about Ireland. Guess he came from there originally."

"No," said Flannelmouth, "never been there. But he likes to talk about the place. Full of the stories."

"So how's he doing?" asked Father Greg.

"Having kind of a hard time. I got him to eat a little breakfast this morning. That's part of the problem. He don't have much of an appetite."

"Is he able to move around, you know, get up?"

"We try to get him up to go to the bathroom back there. But he don't seem interested in doing much except sleep. But the Irish stories, that's different." She had a delighted expression on her face.

Tamara checked two plastic bags hanging above the man, flicked the line leading from one, picked up litter off the long bed table, and disappeared.

The man stirred a little.

"Seamus?" said Father Greg.

The eyes flickered open for just a second. In a moment they opened again.

"Dad?" Flannelmouth cleared his throat.

"Huh?"

"Dad, it's me, Vernal."

The man squinted, trying to focus. "Vernal? What brings you here, lad?"

"You do, dad, Heard you were laid up in the hospital."

"Hate these places. What you doing here? You should be in school."

"Came to see you, dad. Wanted to make sure they were treating you right." Flannelmouth's eyes were getting moist.

"Hate this place. Stick needles in you. Get me out of here."

"Can't do that, dad. You're sick. Got to get you well." Flannelmouth took the gaunt hand in his and started rubbing it gently with the other.

"Good boy, Vernie." He looked up at the father. "Who's he? He a doctor? Get me out of here, doc."

"This is my friend Father Morgan. I stay with him."

"Priest, huh? Getting ready to give me last rites, are they? I'm not dead yet, young man."

"Other kind, dad. Episcopal. He's just a friend."

"Oh," and the head sank back on the pillow, and the eyes closed.

Flannelmouth looked up at the father, not sure what to do.

"Maybe time to go. We can come back." Then, "Mr. Finnegan, we'll let you rest for now. Nice to meet you."

The eyes opened for an instant. "O.K," and he was off to dreamland again. The two stood there for a few minutes, then turned and went out. No sound coming from the other side of the curtain around bed number one.

On the trip back to town, Flannelmouth looked out the window a lot. The father decided to leave him be.

Chapter 8.

The watch.

Avarice is not a vice one would be inclined to associate with Flannelmouth Finnegan. There were those -- schoolteachers and probation officers, for example -- who bemoaned the young man's failure to have absorbed such lessons of our greedy, time-driven civilization. They might use such epithets as "lacking ambition" and "chronically tardy," but the message was clear: The youth was sadly out of step with the spirit of the times. But, alas, even our Flannelmouth could fall sway at times.

It was early on a Saturday afternoon late in July, a time Father Greg usually spent in preparing the sermon for the next day's service, that Flannelmouth went walking along West 14th Street, admiring the merchandise in shop windows as he passed. It was not with any desire to own the objects on display. He was content merely to gaze at their beauty and move on. Until, that is, he noticed a particularly handsome wristwatch in the window of the neighborhood Kmart store.

The watch locked onto the youth and would not let him go. Perhaps it was the challenge to his ingenuity as much as the value of the item in question that drew Flannelmouth closer to study the watch in detail. Oh, how it shone in the artificial sunlight cast on it from somewhere above the top of the window. The more he gazed at the object, the more it called out to him. "Take me with you, I am yours forever." It became all mixed up in the poor lad's head with memories of the lady Pamela.

*

He is in a cabin in the deep woods. Outside a ferocious storm is raging. There is a knocking at the door. It is she of his dreams, pleading for him to let her in, but he says he must not. Again the knocking at the door. Oh please let me in, she pleads. Again he refuses. And yet a third time the knocking at the door. At last he relents and opens the door. She is in his arms and wanting to do naughty things as the door closes behind her. She is his at last. Of a sudden the door flies open and the father comes at him to do vengeance.

Flannelmouth woke up unsettled. Sunday morning. Warm and promising to be a scorcher with high humidity. He went about the washing and dressing mechanically. Breakfast the same. Down the corridor he could hear Father Greg's snoring.

As he waited for the Corrigans to whisk him off to early mass at St. Matthews, he wondered how his dad was doing. The old man seemed so weak. Not like the old days when the man always had a big smile and a bit of an Irish tune and a tale to tell. He wondered about death, still something of an abstraction when it came to humans. He should check Mr. Rat's grave some time.

The Corrigans were like a clock. Seven-thirty, and the green SUV pulled up outside the church. Mrs. Corrigan waved to Flannelmouth. "Hi, Vernal. How are you?

Going to be a hot one today." Or nice one, or rainy one. Like a recording. There were times when he mimicked the lady for Father Greg's benefit.

He climbed into the middle seat, waving to the kids in the back as he did.

"Seat belt, Vernal." Mr. Corrigan never started off without the belt in place.

"Oh, yeah, sorry," and he pulled the strap over and locked it in place. Everybody in the family was a little on the plump side. Mr. Corrigan, whose ruddy neck pushed over the top of his collar. Mrs. Corrigan with her blond curls and big boobs. And the kids, Jeremy, age six, and Peter, age four. Mr. Corrigan sold insurance and Mrs. Corrigan worked in an office somewhere.

"Going to be a hot one," said Mrs. Corrigan to nobody in particular.

"Did you take your car in to get that brake problem attended to?" asked Mr. Corrigan.

"Oh, thanks for reminding me, dear."

There as a grumpy "hmph" from Mr. Corrigan. Meanwhile, a commotion in the back. Peter let out a howl, and Jeremy said, "Cry baby. Here's your Ned's Head."

"Quiet back there," said Mrs. Corrigan, twisting around.

So it went. Typical Sunday morning. Flannelmouth looked out the window at the rows of houses with their manicured lawns. His mind was elsewhere. On a wristwatch, to be precise.

The SUV nosed into a parking space behind the church, and everybody got out into the rising temperature and humidity. There were lots of greetings and "This is our friend, Vernal, yes you remember..., " as the family entered the church. The boys were escorted downstairs, and the adults and their passenger went on into the cavernous sanctuary. The organ was playing, and up front a couple of altar boys, a bit younger than Flannelmouth, were running back and forth setting things up. The choir was beginning to gather over to the left. Flannelmouth liked to listen to the organ. He pretty well tuned everything else out.

As the mass began, he automatically fell into the routine along with the rest of the congregation, which filled about half the pews. Eleven o'clock mass, the place would be full. Meanwhile, he was visualizing the inside of the Kmart store and hatching a strategy step by step.

After mass, Mrs. Corrigan said to Flannelmouth, "We're taking the children to the park. Would you care to join us?"

"No, thank you ma'am. I have a few errands I need to do. Could you drop me off on West 14th? Over near the Kmart would do fine."

"Can you get back home from there?"

"Oh yes, ma'am. I often do."

As he climbed out of the SUV, Flannelmouth said, "See you next week. Thank you for the ride." He waved as they drove off, Jeremy waving back.

Inside the Kmart, business was a little slow. Flannelmouth wandered around until he came to a display of small digital cameras. One had been separated from its cable and lay face up on the counter.

He quickly picked it up and slipped it into his pocket. Nearby a man with a shopping bag was looking over a rack of neckties. Flannelmouth bumped up against the man as he passed, dropping the camera into the shopping bag.

"Oops, oh excuse me, sir."

"No problem," and the man went back to fingering a paisley tie hanging from the rack. Flannelmouth walked to a place where he had a clear view of the checkout counters but the clerks were unlikely to notice him, and waited.

Eventually the man went into one of the checkout lanes. As he was on his way out, an alarm started beeping loudly. He walked back toward the cashier, but the alarm kept beeping. O.K., no gate, alarm stays on, Flannelmouth observed.

On a Saturday afternoon in early August, a young man in his mid-teens walked into the Kmart store on West 14th Street. Later, he would remember having to walk around a group of people carrying signs that said 'No more nukes' and 'Remember Hiroshima' in order to get into the store. A policeman was arguing with one of the marchers.

Inside, the lad wandered past the display cases with seeming aimlessness. Electronics were located right next to men's jewelry. Flannelmouth examined cell phones, digital cameras, and pocket radios, all securely lashed to the counter with cables. His attention, however, was on the adjacent display of cufflinks, tie pins, and, indeed, wristwatches.

A young store clerk snapping bubblegum and winding her finger through her long hair was busy on a cell phone, easily distracted from the wristwatches and other items under her charge. Flannelmouth studied her movements carefully. Just then a man came up, surveyed the wristwatches inside the glass display case, and pointed at a particular one. Out it came, along with several other watches with which it shared a long plastic tray. He appeared to be asking a question to which the young woman lacked the answer. As she turned to reach for the intercom, Flannelmouth brushed past the man, knocking him off balance momentarily.

"Watch it, kid."

"Oh, sorry sir. Here, let me help you."

"Never mind. Jesus, kids are so goddam clumsy."

The young woman turned back to attend to the customer, who by this time had calmed down. "The manager will be here in a minute, sir."

Neither the clerk, the customer, nor the manager, who arrived shortly afterward, noticed an empty spot near the end of the tray when it was returned to the display case ten minutes later.

Flannelmouth headed for the men's room. He ducked inside one of the two open stalls, drew the door shut, and locked it. Next, the watch was extracted from its plastic case. It was a beauty, bejeweled border around the face standing out from the gold frame. "Made in Germany" was etched into the back. Attached to the underside of the watchband was a very small, thin white plastic strip. Flannelmouth tried in vain to detach the strip. Shrugging, he put the watch on his wrist and buckled the strap.

The room was deserted as he left the stall. He quickly stuffed the plastic case under the crumpled paper towels in the trash bin next to the row of sinks and went out.

Back out on the main floor he noticed a woman pushing a stroller with one hand and dragging a resistant toddler with the other. Every once in a while the woman would give a yank on the child's arm, setting off a loud protest from the latter.

The woman was working her way toward the kitchenware department, and Flannelmouth worked right along with her at a distance of a few feet. As she looked over toaster ovens, Flannelmouth went to where electric timers were on display, picked one up, and checked to see if anybody was watching. He approached the lady. "Fine looking child, ma'am," he said, as he walked by. The woman nodded with a little smile. "Thank you -- Dessie stop that." Another yank on the child's arm and the predictable response. The lady looked at her watch, then said, "God, we've got to get going. Come on, Dessie, stop that."

When things had calmed down enough to proceed, the lady headed for the line of checkout counters, unaware that the pocket hanging from the back of the stroller held an electric timer.

Flannelmouth went over near the checkout section and began admiring a number of barbecue grills. As the harassed lady with the stroller and the toddler approached one of the checkout stalls, Flannelmouth moved in behind her. She paid her bill and started to push the stroller the rest of the way through the lane. The alarm began beeping loudly. The poor lady looked around in puzzlement as the alarm kept beeping, and a security guard stepped forward. In the confusion, nobody paid much attention to a young lad walking out empty-handed.

Not given especially to punctuality, Flannelmouth had no particular need for a watch. When he got home, he stowed his new acquisition in the drawer under his bed, right on top of the now-forgotten book of love poems. And there it sat, a veritable ticking time bomb.

Chapter 9.

Alone.

The news came in a phone message for Father Greg. "We are sorry to advise you that Mr. Seamus Finnegan passed away at 2:14 am today. Please contact our social services department at your earliest convenience."

The father turned away from his desk and sat looking out the window, wondering how best to break the news to Flannelmouth. Ah well, just say it right out.

"Flannelmouth," he called down the stairwell.

The lad came out of his room. "Yes, father?"

What now? Had he discovered the watch? Maybe another intruder in the kitchen.

"Would you come up here a minute?"

Flannelmouth came into the office. The father nodded to him to sit down and searched the boy's face. "It's your dad, son."

No matter how much warning a person has had, and there were plenty of them in Seamus's case, it is inevitably a shock to the system.

"Oh," said the lad, and, his face a blank slate, he looked first at one corner of the room, then at the other, then back again. Whatever might be churning through him at that moment, it didn't show. It was rather a dead feeling more than anything. Empty of emotion. Empty of anything.

"Did they say what happened, father?"

"He died early this morning, about two. I don't have any details. I'm supposed to call social services at the hospital."

"I should have been visiting him more." Since the first meeting in the hospital room, there had been only a couple of brief visits. On neither occasion had they been able to wake the man up, he was so heavily medicated.

"It wouldn't have helped. As it was, I told the aide to make sure he knew we'd been there every time we went. He knew you cared."

Flannelmouth got up to go, a little unsteady on his feet. The father came over and put his arms around the boy, who collapsed in a fit of sobbing that couldn't stop. Father Greg led him over to the sofa and sat down next to him. Gradually Flannelmouth settled down and just lay up against the father.

"You O.K.?"

Flannelmouth nodded.

"I'll call social services at the hospital."

He went to his desk, picked up the phone, craned his neck to read the number taped to the wall, and tapped it in on the keypad. Flannelmouth sat whimpering softly and staring at nothing in particular.

"Social services, please." The father could be all business when he needed to. "Yes, I'll wait.... Hello, social services? This is Father Gregory Morgan, St. Luke's.... Morgan, M-O- R.... Yes, that's right.... Yes, I'm calling about Seamus Finnegan. We got a call during the night that he had died.... Finnegan. Seamus Finnegan.... Yes, I'll wait.... Ms. Jenkins? Yes, Ms. Jenkins, I'm calling about Seamus Finnegan. We got a call.... Yes, I know, thank you...thank you.... I have the man's son here with me.... Vernal, V-E.... Yes, that's right.... He's fourteen. He's the only living relative as far as we know. There was a daughter who was adopted out in infancy, but nobody knows of her whereab.... Right. Yes, exactly. Could somebody meet with us this morning?" He swung around in the desk chair and nodded to Flannelmouth. Still on the phone, "Ten thirty? Yes, we'll be there.... Yes, I know where you're located. Third floor, main building, right?... Thank you, Ms. Jenkins.... Yes, O.K., thanks. Goodbye."

Flannelmouth had regained a little of his equilibrium by the time they got to the hospital. The father led the way to the bank of elevators and pressed the up button. In a couple of minutes the door opened, and an orderly pushed a woman on a gurney out, then held the door until they were inside.

"Let's see," said the father as they left the elevator, "social services, yes, a few doors down this way on the right."

They sat waiting in the reception room, neither one saying anything. Flannelmouth in something of a daze. Ms. Jenkins finally emerged from a corridor. Colored lady. On the plump side. Beautiful eyes.

"Yes, Father Morgan, and this must be Vernal. Oh, I'm so sorry." It seemed genuine enough. She shook the boy's hand. The next few minutes were sort of a blur.

They were now sitting across the desk from the lady in a cramped office overflowing with forms of various sorts and stacks of bulging manila folders. Behind her was a computer.

Ms. Jenkins was checking a record. Then her eyes came up to meet theirs. She looked from one to the other. "Did anybody fill you in on any of the details?'

The father shook his head. "All we got was a phone message that he died at 2:14."

"O.K.," checking back in the record, "yes, the nurse came by on his rounds at 1:40. He'd been O.K. up to then. The nurse noticed problems, and they put him on code immediately. The team tried to resuscitate, but it was too late.

"Vernal, he never woke up through any of it." She reached over and took his hand. "He didn't suffer. Hear what I'm saying. He never new any of this."

They sat like that for a few minutes, nobody saying anything.

Father Greg asked, "Did they say last rites?"

"I don't know, father. It doesn't say here. I can check if you'd like."

"No, that's O.K. Oh, I'm an Episcopal priest. The court has the boy staying with me. It's a little complicated."

Ms. Jenkins nodded. "O.K., well, there are a few details. Do you want to sit in on this, Vernal, or...?"

"That's O.K., ma'am. You and the father can deal with that." She released his hand and he started to get up. Father Greg looked over at him with a worried expression. Flannelmouth shook him off. "I'm O.K. Oh, ma'am, you got a bathroom I could use?"

"Just across from where you came in and a little way down. By the way, we have cocoa in the staff lounge -- that room on the left just as you came in. Where the tables are."

"Actually I was wondering if you have some coffee."

"Oh, well yes, uh," and she looked over to the father.

"Yes, it's O.K. He drinks coffee."

"O.K., that's in the same place, Vernal."

Five minutes later, Flannelmouth was sitting in the staff lounge nursing a cup of coffee and listening to two women chatting at the corner table. It was an old habit that kicked in from time to time. Once a survival mechanism, now it was more just habit.

"So I said to the teacher, 'When he's in school he's your problem.' She didn't like that too much. Next year I'm looking for a charter."

"Yeah, its bad. My sister teaches at Jefferson. God, those kids walk all over the teachers, and they can't lay a hand on them. Oh, you and Carl going to that theater festival in Canada this year? With gas so high, I think we'll stay closer to home. Jimmy's in camp for a couple of weeks...."

It was a world Flannelmouth knew only from a distance. From the beginning, school was one long series of transfers. It was rarely that he finished the school year with the same teacher he had started with in the fall. And now with his dad gone, the last vestige of anything approaching a family was gone, too. He wondered about the sister he had never seen. Who knew where she was? He might run into her on the street some day and not even know it.

His mind kept running in circles. The two women had left. A man was at another table, eating a sandwich and doing a crossword puzzle. Flannelmouth went over and poured himself another cup of coffee. He knew he shouldn't. It gave him the jitters sometimes.

Father Greg came into the lounge. "Hi, guy. You must be famished. We can eat in the cafeteria."

"Whatever, father." Flannelmouth was ready to let somebody else do the driving.

"I got a lot of information. We'll talk and then I'll get back with Ms. Jenkins."

"She's a nice lady."

"Well she said some nice things about you, too. If you ever need to talk to somebody -- I mean, besides me -- she'll be glad to talk with you."

He salted away the information. She'd be a hell of a lot better to deal with than that probation lady, Pat.

In the afternoon, they sat at the kitchen table and went over things. Flannelmouth had to be brought back into the conversation from time to time.

"One thing Ms. Jenkins asked about was relatives. Know anybody on either side of the family that might still be around?"

"My dad's folks both died some years ago. He had some brothers and sisters, but they kind of gave up on him with the drink and all. I have no idea what's happened to any of them. He never talked about them anyway. I don't know too much about my mom's family except she came from up in New England somewhere. My dad said the family threw her out when she married him. Wouldn't have anything to do with her."

"Didn't like the Irish, huh?"

"Not so much that. According to him, it was him being Catholic, you know. Oh, there was the mom's sister, Theresa. She's the one took my sister away and got her adopted out when my mom died. That was the end of Theresa as far as my dad was concerned."

"All right, so there's no family I guess." The father was busy writing notes and didn't look up.

Something about the way the father said it hit Flannelmouth in a way it hadn't before. There was no family any more. Not a soul. He was all alone. It made him shiver.

The father noticed. "Not easy," he said. "It'll take time to get used to it. I'm so glad you had a chance to see him."

Flannelmouth wasn't sure how he felt about it. Father Greg shifted onto less freighted ground. "We have to talk about the funeral and the burial. Any thoughts? No rush, son."

"He'd want a proper burial, father."

"Catholic, I assume."

"Oh yes, that he would. He was of the faith, though he didn't always measure up, you know."

"...And a funeral mass, I guess."

"Oh that, too, father."

"What about the church the Corrigans take you to?"

"Oh, I don't know, that's a pretty fancy church. My dad wouldn't have felt comfortable there."

"That shouldn't make any difference. Well, think about it."

Which is what Flannelmouth did for the rest of the day. By dinnertime he still hadn't come up with anything. Then in the middle of macaroni and cheese he said, "The sisters."

"Sisters? What sisters?" asked the father.

"The Saint Francis folks."

"O.K., what about them?"

"They knew my dad. Sister Patrice there especially."

"You want them to do the funeral mass?" Father Greg was trying to catch up.

"They have seminary students come to help out. Maybe one of them knows how to do the mass."

"Well I don't know. Would that be a proper one?"

Flannelmouth gave it some thought. Then, "I think it would for my dad, Father."

"Well, O.K., we'll give it a try."

He picked up the phone and looked for the number on the list on the wall. "I should let them know about Seamus anyway."

There was a little wait after he punched in the number. "Hello, this is Father Morgan, St. Luke's. We were over there.... Yes, that's the one. I'm wondering if Sister Patrice Ann is.... Well, yes, that's part of why I called.... Yes, during the night.... Yes, thank you, I'll let him know.... Yes, I'll wait." He rested the phone against his stomach, and the two of them sat looking at each other.

"She wanted you to know how sorry she is."

He put the phone back against his ear. "Hello.... Hello, Sister.... Yes, that's right, about two o'clock this morning.... No, he may not have even been aware what was happening.... Yes, I agree.... Sister, we wanted to let you know about Seamus of course, but there was something else. The son wanted to know if we might hold the funeral mass there.... Yes, at your place.... I know, I said the same thing, but he, well, he thought his dad might have preferred.... Of course. No, I know you don't. But we were wondering if one of the seminarians might.... the ones who come and volunteer.... Tell you what, why don't we drop by tomorrow morning and talk about it? You might also know about churches in the area.... Ten? O.K., we'll come by then. Goodbye till then.... Yes, bye now."

They had been waiting for about twenty minutes in Sister Patrice Ann's office when she walked in and sat in the desk chair facing them.

"Sorry for the delay," she said, "It's been one of those mornings." Then to Flannelmouth, "I'm so sorry about your dad. He'll be missed. A jolly spirit, that one."

He nodded but said nothing.

"About this funeral mass, could you say a little more about what you have in mind?" Then turning to the father before the lad could answer, "Oh, before I forget it, is there a funeral home involved?"

"Not yet. That's one of the things Ms. Jenkins mentioned. She's the social worker at county hospital."

"We know a good one," said Sister Patrice Ann. "Devlin's. We've used them before. Did Ms. Jenkins say anything about the cost?

"Yes, we talked about that. There's the standard $750 welfare pays for handling the body and the burial. Do you happen to know what Devlin charges?"

"Yes, $750. Of course they will charge more if you want anything more than the minimum."

As so often happened, the adults were leaving Flannelmouth out of the conversation.

He broke in. "My dad would want a proper burial...."

"Yes, of course," said the sister. "We have spaces reserved at the Catholic cemetery on Ridge. He would go in one of those. There would be a simple marker at the site."

"...And a proper funeral."

"Oh yes, you were thinking one of our young seminarians might celebrate the mass?"

"Yes, ma'am."

The sister shook her head, "We can certainly arrange to do it in our chapel here, but I'm sorry, son. Only a priest can do that -- one of the Roman Catholic kind," and she smiled as her gaze shifted to Father Greg, who nodded.

The sister went on. "I think we can find us a priest to celebrate the mass. Father Daly's not far away. He came to administer last rites to a man who was shot a few doors down from here last spring. Would that do, son?"

Flannelmouth nodded. Whatever.

Sister Patrice Ann took a cell phone out of her pocket and began dialing. A short wait, then, "Hello, this is Sister Patrice Ann at...yes, hello, is this...? Yes, Father, fine, and the same to you. I was wondering if...oh, I'm sorry.... Yes, if you would, please. You have the number, I believe.... Very good. If you would, then. Thank you Father.... Yes, thank you.... Good bye."

"He was in the middle of a meeting. He'll get back to me in a little bit. The only question will be the location. He will probably want it at his church. Would that be O.K., son?"

Flannelmouth took a minute to answer. "I'd like it here, ma'am." The tone was resolute.

Sister Patrice Ann nodded. "I'll see what I can do, son."

So, step by step, the preparations for Seamus Finnegan's final farewell went forward. Death is such a complicated business, thought Flannelmouth, I wish it was over. He thought about the countless hearses he had seen passing by on the street followed by cars with white pennants fluttering above them and the TV mayhem in which people were mowed down with abandon and 9/11 and wars in the Middle East. In every case, somebody had to make funeral arrangements and say their goodbyes and weep and feel empty and weep again and feel empty again and yet again. It was all quite overwhelming. But then, death had never been such an intimate acquaintance for our young friend, not since his mother had passed away, and he understood so little of that at the time.

On a steamy summer afternoon in the small chapel at the mission known as Sisters of St. Francis, Father Brian Daly of the Church of the Blessed Virgin celebrated the funeral mass for Seamus Finnegan. A small gathering of people was there to see him on his way. Three men with some kind of longshoremen's insignia on their overalls sat a little apart from the rest of the group.

At the end, Father Daly asked if any in attendance would like to make any comments.

There was a pause of several minutes, then "He was my friend. I will miss his friendly spirit." Another pause, and "Seamus would give his last quarter to anybody who needed it -- or the rest of his drink, for that matter." Laughter rattled through the room. One of the longshoremen said, "Aye, Seamus was a good worker when he was sober enough not to fall in the drink." That set off a big laugh.

People settled down as Sister Patrice Ann spoke up. "He was one of God's children. He hated no man on this earth."

Flannelmouth wiped his eyes on his sleeve. "I loved you, dad."

After a little more time, Father Daly signaled the end of the mass, and the group dispersed. In turn, each person came and shook Flannelmouth's hand on the way out. Then Father Daly, Father Greg, Flannelmouth, and Sister Patrice Ann went to Father Greg's car to follow the waiting hearse to St. Mary's Cemetery, located in a gritty, rundown suburb just over the city line.

Nobody said anything until Sister Patrice Ann spoke up, "Thank you, father, that was a beautiful service," and the others nodded.

"I agree," said Father Daly. "I must say that was an unusual setting, but we meet new challenges every day in this business, don't we?"

The hearse led the way into the cemetery and around to a freshly dug grave. Two men with shovels were waiting for them. Father Greg parked the Honda behind the ambulance, and the passengers climbed out in silence while the casket was unloaded and taken to graveside, where it was positioned above the excavation.

Father Daly sprinkled holy water on the casket, intoned "I am the resurrection and the life," and signaled to the waiting men. The casket was slowly lowered into the grave until it disappeared from view. Flannelmouth had a fleeting impulse to jump in after it, then let out a long breath and was still.

"If any would care to put a handful of earth in, they may do it now," said Father Daly. Sister Patrice Ann stepped forward, scooped up a handful from the mound next to the grave, and tossed into the hole. Father Greg did the same. Flannelmouth hesitated, then stepped up. The earth was cool and soft in his hand. As he got to the edge of the opening, it seemed like such a very long way down. The earth thudded against the lid of the casket.

People began moving away from the site. As Flannelmouth was climbing into the father's car, the image of Mr. Rat's little grave behind the church flashed into his mind for an instant.

Dinner that night was a simple affair. Neither of them said anything at first, then Father Greg said, "That was a good send-off for Seamus."

Flannelmouth nodded.

"So what are your thoughts just now?" asked the father.

The other took a long time in answering. "He let me down."

"What do you mean?"

"He was never there when I needed him. Too busy with the drink to look after his family." It came out in a gush mixed with sobs. The lad's head went down on the table, barely missing his plate, and his body heaved in silence.

Father Greg reached over and patted the shaking head.

Flannelmouth was done with eating. He got up and went to his room and lay down. The father decided to let him be. In the darkness, the youth wondered what was to become of him. The father would soon be married to Pamela, probably move to a distant suburb to raise a family. There was nobody else. Flannelmouth saw only a long tunnel, one that he would have to traverse alone.

Chapter 10.

A Chance Discovery.

Things settled down after that, and the routines took over. As the start of school approached, Flannelmouth was looking forward to it. His sessions with Jim Landry had revealed a level of aptitude that had been noticeably missing in the past.

He was now an essential player in the weekly food handout. Volunteers would often ask him where something was located. Everybody knew him as Flannelmouth. The unusual monicker only helped to make him something of a celebrity, especially among young children who accompanied their parents to pick up groceries. That was all to end soon.

One Wednesday morning as Flannelmouth lay on his bed thinking of nothing in particular, Father Greg popped his head in the door.

"I have to go check out a silver pattern Pam likes. Be back in a couple of hours."

Flannelmouth waved to him as he disappeared down the corridor. Absentmindedly, the youth opened the drawer under his bed and pulled out the watch. As he lay turning it this way and that, catching a glint here and there, he glimpsed Pat Spetrino walking by outside. He quickly opened the drawer, and tossed the watch in, and pushed it shut.

"Where's Father Morgan? And what did you just put in the drawer there?"

"What's what?" Panic seized him.

"Whatever you just shoved in the drawer."

"Oh nothing, just some stuff I keep in there."

She stepped over to where he was lying, reached down and yanked the drawer open. "What's this?"

"Just a watch."

She picked it up and said, "Where'd you get it."

All he could think of was Middleburg. Calling upon well-ingrained survival skills from the past, "Oh, that's from the father. He said he wanted me to have something to remember him by. You know, me going to some other home eventually."

"Oh, and what's this under it?"

"That was from the father also. He's been wanting me to improve my reading skills. I'm going to start school soon."

"I see," and she started flipping through the first few pages.

In an instant she'd pulled her cell phone out of her purse, flipped it open, and was dialing a number. Something had gone terribly wrong. Flannelmouth waited for the impending doom.

Her back was to him. "Yes, I need an emergency shelter.... Tonight.... No, it can't wait.... Derby? You mean there's nothing closer than that? Crap. O.K., give me the address," and she held the phone between her shoulder and her jaw while she wrote. "Don't bother, I've got a GPS."

She shoved the phone back in her purse.

"Where's the reverend?"

"He went shopping. He said he'd be back in a couple of hours."

"O.K., we'll deal with him later. Get your things. You're coming with me. Is this your bag?" She was holding the old Middleburg laundry bag open and stuffing clothes into it.

"But I want to talk to the father." He was close to tears.

"No. Never mind the father right now. Come on, move it."

Flannelmouth was crying as he gathered up the rest of his belongings and handed them to her. She took a quick look around the room. "Is this everything?"

He nodded and wiped his eyes with his sleeve. Pat said, "Stay here. I'll be back in few minutes."

She went out into the corridor and was soon on the phone, talking with somebody so quietly that Flannelmouth couldn't tell what she was saying. He sat on his bed weeping softly.

A few minutes later she came back in the room, grabbed him by the arm. and dragged him out and down the corridor, while he held tightly to his worldly possessions.

All the way to Derby, Flannelmouth fired questions at his captor. "Where are you taking me? Why can't I see Father Greg? What's this all about, anyway?"

Her eyes were on the road and the GPS. The answers didn't really answer anything.

"Never mind. You're going to be in an emergency shelter for now. The DA will probably want to talk to you."

"But the father doesn't know where I am."

"He will soon enough."

As Greg Morgan pulled up next to the church he noticed a police car across the street. All he could think of was that somebody had broken in. Then, "Flannelmouth! Is he back in trouble again?"

He dashed down the metal stairs to find the door standing ajar. Inside were a police officer and a man in a brown suit, chatting in the corridor outside his room.

"What happened?" he demanded.

"Are you Reverend Morgan?" asked the man in the suit.

"Yes. What's going on? Did somebody break in?"

"Nobody broke in. We need to talk with you. You need to come down to headquarters."

"Did something happen to Flan...Vernal?"

"Vernal is O.K. He's being moved. We have some questions we have to ask you."

"Would somebody mind telling me what's going on?"

"Sorry, sir. There's a little matter we need to discuss with you. Please come with us, sir."

Totally puzzled, Father Greg followed the two of them out to the waiting cruiser.

"He what?" The father tried to make some sense out of it all. The cluster of people around him didn't help.

"He says you gave him an expensive watch and a book. You have a right to remain silent." It was the big guy in the brown suit.

"I don't need to remain silent. Am I being charged with something?" He was completely baffled.

"Did you give him a watch?"

"No. Christ, what is this?"

"Did you give him a book?"

"We've given him lots of books -- math, English, social studies. The kid has a lot of catch up to do before school starts." Settling down a little now. "Listen, I have a right to know what this is all about. I repeat, am I being charged with something?"

"We're not at liberty to say, sir."

"O.K., I'm not at liberty to discuss this without consulting my lawyer. Excuse me. gentlemen," and he got up to leave. "Would somebody take me back to St. Luke's?"

"Yessir. Conley, would you take the reverend back to his church?"

"But lieutenant, we...."

The man in the brown suit shook his head. Then to Father Greg, "Reverend, we may need to talk with you again. Will you be at the church for the next day or two?"

"Of course. Look, I know you guys have to do your job. But there's been some kind of terrible mix-up."

"Thank you, reverend. You're right. Just doing our job."

Half an hour later, "Is Steve Cohen in? This is Greg Morgan. Tell him it's urgent. Yes, I'll wait." Time was slowing to a crawl for Father Greg.

Finally, "Hi, Greg, what's up? Did they catch you messing with the choir girls or something?"

"Don't joke. This is serious. Flannelmouth -- he's the young kid I told you about.... Yes, that's the one. They moved him out of here without telling me. I just came back from police headquarters. They were asking me about some things I was supposed to have given him. The whole thing is crazy. Could you check it out for me?"

"What kind of things?"

"A wristwatch, which I know zip about, and a book. Have no idea what that's about."

"Maybe he stole them. You said he had a long record of that sort of thing."

"No, I'm sure not.

"O.K., I'll see what's up and get back to you."

It was late afternoon before Steve called.

"Well." Come on Steve, don't stop there.

"Well what?"

"Seems your young friend had a very expensive wristwatch and a book of erotic poetry -- as in *homo*erotic -- stashed in his room at your place. Said they were gifts from you. So now the county is trying to hang a child predator charge on you."

"No, I don't believe it. That couldn't be."

"All I can tell you is they have the items in their possession. They didn't just conjure them up. Listen, I know you have faith in the goodness of humankind and all that other bullshit, but it looks like your little friend did a job on you."

Long pause, then Greg said, "Get back to me when you know something."

"Will do. Take care."

Greg didn't bother to answer before he hung up.

He was furious; furious at Steve and furious at the police and furious at the probation department and furious at the world in general.

It wasn't until he got up in the middle of the night to pee that furious spilled over onto Flannelmouth and eventually onto himself.

"What a stupid jerk I was to trust that kid." Sleep was out of the question. He thrashed around for the rest of the night, his mind running in circles.

*

The couple who ran the group home in Derby were as uncommunicative as Pat Spetrino. The woman seemed kindly enough, but if she knew anything, she wasn't sharing it.

Pat's parting words to the couple had been, "Don't let him out of your sight. He tends to run if he gets the chance."

And they made sure one of them was with Flannelmouth or close by every minute.

Hi Vernal Mr. Cobb and I will make sure your stay here is comfortable this is your room you will share it with Robert this is your bed you can put your things in that chest at the foot there or on the shelf there here is the bathroom for the two of you shower sink toilet everything here are your towel and washcloth meals are breakfast at seven sharp morning chores you'll be on kitchen detail see here is your name on the list on the kitchen door lunch at noon we'll be eating lunch soon and dinner at six see here the meal times are posted on this sign on the door of your room and here is a bible in the drawer of the table next to your bed this box by the window has a rope ladder in case of fire hah hah haven't had any fires in the thirty years we've been here we're in that room down the hall there is another bedroom on this floor and two more up on the third floor....

Flannelmouth heard it but didn't hear it. Normally he would be sizing up the place, figuring out an escape route; maybe the rope ladder. But he had run out of steam and was just waiting for things to happen.

*

He throws the wristwatch oh cursed wristwatch down in the big hole in the ground, and a hundred crows fly up out of the hole, and they try to peck his eyes out, and he throws the book oh cursed book down in the big hole in the ground, and a hundred and yet more hundreds of crows fly up out of the hole and try to peck his eyes out, and it never ends, and it will never end.

Flannelmouth awoke in a sweat. Total darkness in the room and Robert's even breathing close by. He couldn't sleep, and his left leg kept twitching, keeping him awake. So it went until the pale block of light high above them told him it was early dawn. Never having cared about time before, now he desperately wanted to know what time it was. How long before we get up?

Gradually it got lighter, and he could make out bureaus and other objects in the room. He was up and dressed when Robert stirred awake. The kid had red hair and freckles. Sort of skinny.

"Hi, what's your name."

"Flannelmouth."

"Flannel what?"

"Mouth. Flannelmouth."

"Christ, what a funny name."

On top of everything else, Flannelmouth was sure he was not going to like Robert.

"So what happened?" Robert was also nosy.

"Search me. They yanked me out of where I was and put me in here. I was in a church in the city. St. Luke's."

"Weird. My mom was beating up on my little sister, and they took us all out and put us in different homes. I don't know where anybody is."

"You got a dad?"

"Prison. He slashed a guy with a knife. They got into fight. Well, the guy deserved it."

"Oh." Flannelmouth wanted to turn the guy off.

"Come on, I'll show you about breakfast."

Flannelmouth followed Robert downstairs to the dining room, where other guys were getting cereal and juice and loading up the four-slot toaster. The two colored kids didn't talk to anybody.

"Yeah, this is Flannelmouth, everybody." Robert tending out on his new roommate.

A couple other kids were new. Flannelmouth forgot their names as soon as he heard them. Seemed to be a lot of coming and going in this place.

"Any coffee?" asked Flannelmouth. Robert said no, the Cobbs didn't serve it.

So he sat at breakfast and poked his food and ate little. He kept yawning and let other people do the talking.

A man he assumed was Mr. Cobb came out of the kitchen and checked the juice and milk pitchers. He came over and sat next to Flannelmouth. "Hi, Vernal, I'm Mr. Cobb. We got you on kitchen duty today. You and Luis over there," pointing at a darkish boy sitting by himself.

Flannelmouth nodded. He had nothing to say to the man. He wondered what was happening with Father Greg. Mr. Cobb sat as if he expected the boy to say something, then got up and went back into the kitchen.

Kitchen duty started off with putting the milk, juice, butter, and jam in the fridge, clearing dishes, and putting them in the dishwasher. Luis waited for instructions and followed them at a deliberate pace. He was obviously in no hurry. A couple of times Mrs. Cobb had to move dishes Flannelmouth had put in the dishwasher the wrong way. Her explanations fell on deaf ears. His mind was a blank.

The rest of the day was a blur. He cut vegetables and threw things in pots and cut cheese with a wire thing and whatever else he was told. Where was Luis? Who cared? Flannelmouth was a well-oiled machine going through the motions. Lunch came and went. Soccer in the yard out back. It was easy to become invisible at soccer while others raced around and got excited.

Dinner. More clean up. TV. Bed.

Bed. He feared sleep more than anything. Sleep, when your imagination broke loose to conjure up terrible images to haunt you.

He's running as fast as he can to get away from the two angry mastiffs close behind. In the rear, urging them on, is the devil surrounded by a huge black cloud. He can feel the mastiffs' hot breath and their fangs nipping at his legs. The scene keeps repeating itself. It will keep on forever.

Flannelmouth woke up. For a moment he was back in his bed at St. Luke's. No, he was at the group home. He wondered if the waking nightmare would ever end.

The next morning, Mrs. Cobb told Flannelmouth he would be going to a meeting in the city.

"What is the meeting about?"

"I don't know anything about it. They just said to get ready."

He was sure she was lying. Everybody knew the truth. Everybody knew what a terrible person he was.

At a quarter to ten, Pat Spetrino came to pick him up.

"What kind of a meeting is this?"

"It's a meeting with the district attorney. He has some questions he wants to ask you."

"About what? What is this all about, anyway?"

"I'm not allowed to say anything. I just have to get you there."

"I have a right to know."

"It's not about you, kid."

"It's about the father, isn't it? You all don't like the father."

"Look, kid, we do our job, you do yours. Your job is to answer some questions, that's all."

Flannelmouth decided on the spot that, if they weren't going to answer his questions, he wasn't going to answer any of theirs.

She drove into an underground garage under the courthouse and parked next to a thick concrete pillar.

"Come on," she said.

He followed her into a small hallway where they stood waiting for an elevator.

They were soon on their way up to the second floor. Flannelmouth steadied himself against the wall of the elevator. The door slid open, revealing a small lobby with a reception desk facing the elevators. Pat took Flannelmouth down a corridor to a small room with a table and several chairs and, off to one side, a desk with a computer.

"Wait here," she said, closing the door behind her as she went out.

Flannelmouth sat down in one of the chairs at the table and sat. And sat. And sat. Finally the doorknob turned, and in came a man in a dark suit. He was followed by a secretary with a legal pad and, behind her, Pat Spetrino. The secretary went and sat down at the desk and booted up the computer.

"Hi, Vernal," said the man, "I'm Jerry Rossi. I'm an assistant district attorney. I have a few questions I'd like to ask you, O.K.?"

Flannelmouth shrugged.

"O.K.," to the secretary, "this is Vernal E. Finnegan, a minor, who until two days ago was residing at St. Luke's Episcopal Church at 1124 Moreland Street with the rector, the Reverend Gregory N. Morgan.

"Vernal, I am going to show you two objects. I want to know if you recognize these objects." He put the watch and the book on the table.

Flannelmouth stared at the man blankly.

"Vernal? These objects here. Do you recognize them?"

The attorney turned to Pat. "This kid got a hearing problem?"

"Not that I'm aware of. Kid, tell Jerry what you told me." The little smirk that had been playing around the edges of the lady's mouth had disappeared.

"If this kid won't talk, we don't have any kind of a case. Your word against his."

"Look, Vernal, just tell the man what you told me." Up a few decibels from before maybe?

One thing for sure. This was about Father Greg, not Flannelmouth. There was something they were trying to pin on the father. Things were beginning to look a little brighter of a sudden. In fact, it occurred to our Flannelmouth that he had them right where he wanted them. Whatever they were trying to hang on Father Greg, without his help they were stuck.

Lawyer Jerry looked at his watch. Lady Pat looked at the ceiling. Flannelmouth looked straight ahead. After a few minutes, the attorney said, "I have a couple of things I have to get to. Let me know if there's any change here, O.K.?"

There was an exasperated 'hmph' from the lady. Meeting over. The trip back to the elevator was rather brisk. Before long they were headed back to the group home. Flannelmouth looked out on the passing scene. Rather enjoying the ride. Not the driver. She was seething.

"You little bastard."

Tut tut, Miss Pat, is that the way probation officers talk? Especially juvenile probation officers?

"I'll have your fanny back in Middleburg so fast it will spin your head right off its axis."

Flannelmouth knew an idle threat when he heard one. It was familiar ground for him. It dawned on him that he was more familiar with this particular ground than the lady.

"O.K., buster, you're going to sit in that group home till you rot."

Even that prospect wasn't looking so bad. Nice folks, those Cobbs. As compared with a few places he'd been, it was right up there on the charts. He might even get himself appointed to kitchen duty permanently. Maybe show them a few dishes he'd learned from the newspaper recipe lady. No, not bad at all. As for the comings and goings of the home's more temporary residents, that had been Flannelmouth's whole life.

The only sour note in this rosy scenario was not knowing what had happened to the father. That was a worry, as well it might be.

*

"Want some good news?" Steve Cohen sounded downright chipper.

"I could use some about now," said Greg Morgan.

"There's been some kind of retraction from your friend Vernal."

"Retraction? What do you mean?"

"Not exactly a retraction. He's refusing to testify now, and without that they don't have any kind case against you. The probation officer says he told her you gave him the items, but now he's refusing to cooperate. So now it's her word against his."

"But they might still come after him for stolen property."

"Might. I didn't pursue that one. Anyway, you're in the clear." They agreed to stay in touch as he hung up the phone.

Greg sat staring at nothing in particular. Good, let the little jerk get what's coming to him.

That lasted well into the afternoon. Then he began having second thoughts, and a feeling of failure swept over him. The kid had such promise. It was still hard to reconcile the Flannelmouth he knew with the evidence they had in hand.

Now a different theory took shape: Pat Spetrino had it in for the two of them. Maybe she planted the stuff on the kid. As far-fetched as the notion was, it was about the only straw worth grabbing for.

Greg's relief at being out from under a legal cloud was short-lived. A few days after getting this news, he received a phone call from the bishop's secretary. Could he come by the diocesan office tomorrow?

"What's on the agenda?"

"I don't know, father. I was just told to set something up. Would two in the afternoon work for you?"

"Yes, I'll be there." Now what was this about? Probably more bad news on next year's budget. They kept slicing a little off the allocation each year.

Promptly at two, he walked into the outer office. He had copies of the last few years' budgets for St. Luke's. Ready for whatever.

As he was ushered into the inner sanctum, he saw a priest he didn't recognize sitting next to Bishop Downing at the conference table.

"Sit down, Greg. This is Father Kilby. I asked him to sit in with us this afternoon."

"Hi," said Greg, as they shook hands and he settled into a seat on the other side of the table. There was something in the way Father Kilby was looking at him that was unsettling.

"What's up?"

"Let me get right to it," said Bishop Downing. "We got a call from the District Attorney's office the other day. Something about a boy who was staying with you at one time."

"Oh that," said Greg smiling. "There was a misunderstanding about some items he said I gave to him."

"Apparently they still have some questions about that."

The smile left Greg's face. "They dropped their investigation. There's no legal action planned. The thing was a total misunderstanding. I'd be glad to explain it."

"Please do," said the bishop. "In the first place, the diocese was unaware that you had a young man living with you."

Totally unprepared for this line of inquiry, Greg fumbled for words.

"O.K. Let me go back a few months. I was at the juvenile court on another case...."

Father Kilby broke in. "Was this concerning one of your parishioners -- this other case?"

"No -- well, yes. You see, we provide a range of community services. There was a teenaged girl who had been brought up on drug charges -- using marijuana -- and her mother asked me to speak in her behalf."

"And was this a family known to your church?"

"They live in the neighborhood. They use the food cupboard."

"Oh, I wasn't aware that our rectors got involved in court cases concerning people outside of the parish."

The bishop stepped in. "St. Luke's is in a very distressed part of the city. They see their mission as including services to the whole neighborhood."

"Oh, yes," said Father Kirby, "well I guess churches vary as to how they see their mission. But I think we're getting off course here. You were in the juvenile court, and...."

Greg felt himself being sucked into a witness role -- witness and accused all wrapped up in one. "Yes, well I -- there was this young man...."

"You had been asked to represent him?"

"Could I just tell what happened?" He could feel his anger rising, and he turned to the bishop for support.

"Yes, go on," said Bishop Downing, waving Father Kilby off.

Greg began unfolding the story of how he met Flannelmouth, how the judge had mistaken him for a Roman Catholic priest, the boy's progress at St. Luke's, and the series of run-ins with Pat Spetrino.

The more he talked, the more he felt things getting out of control. When he got to the part about the watch and the book, he was sure neither man was believing a word he said.

Silence. The silence deepened. Then Bishop Downing spoke. "Greg, I'm sure this has been a major strain for you. We're thinking it might be a good time to take a little break. You've been going at it for several years now without much of a letup. The church does provide for sabbaticals for its priests. We can appoint someone to fill in for you in the interim. What would you think of that?"

"What kind of a break? How long, I mean?"

"A year, maybe."

"Is this a question or a statement?"

The bishop didn't answer but just nodded his head. Greg knew the answer. He pushed his chair back and got up.

"I'll be in touch," he said.

They shook hands and he walked out of the office. In his heart he knew he was walking out of a lot more than that.

Chapter 11.

Redemption.

Flannelmouth had become an essential part of the Cobbs' group home. Considering the life he'd led in earlier years, it was a major triumph. He assisted Mrs. Cobb in the kitchen on a regular basis. Now and then he made little suggestions for improving a casserole with a trace of sage or a dash of cinnamon. When new boys came to the home, it was Flannelmouth's job to explain the kitchen duties to them. They even set him up in his own room on the third floor.

St. Anne's was a couple of blocks away, and he went there for mass every Sunday. Father Thomas talked to him once or twice about becoming an altar boy, but he had no trouble passing up the opportunity. Leave well enough alone, he thought.

In school, he was experiencing a kind of success he'd never known. Some of the other students kidded him about being teacher's pet, but he ignored it. For the most part, he kept to himself and did what was expected. Getting involved with his peers in the past had usually led to trouble of one sort or another, and he planned to steer clear of trouble. Middleburg was never too far from his mind.

It was on a Thursday just after lunch that he overheard a phone conversation that would change all of that. It was between Mrs. Cobb and one of her friends.

"St. Luke's? The church on West....? Oh...." The rest of the conversation was lost as the dishwasher went into a new cycle. But the brief mention he heard yanked Flannelmouth back to the events that had brought him here in the first place. What had happened to the father? He had to know. He brooded on the matter for a full day. Then a thought occurred to him.

The next morning when they had a break from schoolwork, Flannelmouth hunted up the lady of the house.

"Mrs. Cobb, I wonder if I might make a phone call."

"Is it local, dear?"

"Yes, ma'am."

"Oh fine, fine."

"Do you by any chance know the number of the county hospital?"

"Oh it's right here on the bulletin board, dear. Are you feeling sick?"

"No, no, it's about a friend."

He waited until she had left the kitchen, then tried the number.

"Social services. May I help you?"

"I wonder if I might speak with Ms. Jenkins."

"Who shall I say is calling?"

"It's Vernal Finnegan, ma'am."

"Will she know what this is about?"

"Uh, yes, I think so."

Then Ms. Jenkins's voice came on the line. "Flannelmouth? Is that you?" How'd she know the nickname? Must have been part of that conversation when he went out to get a cup of coffee.

"Yes, ma'am. I was wondering if I might come and see you."

"Yes, of course. How've you been doing since, you know, your father passed away? That has to have been hard for you."

"I've been all right, really. Actually it's something else."

"How's Father Morgan these days?"

"That's something I wanted to talk to you about."

"Well, let me see. I assume you're in school now. How about next Monday at four...no make that four-thirty...would you be able to get out here then?"

"I'll have to check and see. If you don't hear from me, I'll see you then, ma'am."

The next Monday, Mr. Cobb drove Flannelmouth to the hospital. Flannelmouth said he could find his way to the social services suite, but Mr. Cobb knew his duty: Don't let this kid out of your sight. So the two of them went to the office on the third floor together.

"Have a seat," said the secretary, looking up from the computer, "she'll be with you in a minute."

Flannelmouth sat idly thumbing through magazines on the table next to him while Mr. Cobb stared at something out the window. In a few minutes, Ms. Jenkins came into view.

"Flannelmouth, how are you?" and she gave him a hug. "And this is...."

"I'm Donald Cobb, miss. Vernal here lives with us."

"Oh, I see," though she didn't. Sensing Flannelmouth's discomfort, she said, "Mr. Cobb, why don't you stay here. There's coffee in the staff room out next to where you came in. I think Flan...Vernal may want to talk with me alone."

"Oh I...." But he read her expression and took a step backward. "I'll see you in a little bit, Vernal."

The youth waved to him and turned to follow Ms. Jenkins to her office.

The place was still as crowded as ever. They sat opposite each other across the desk.

"So you're staying with the Cobbs? Is that like a group home?"

He nodded. Ms. Jenkins sat and waited for more.

"I don't know what's become of the father." He looked on the verge of crying.

"Oh, I thought...."

"They took me away from there. Just picked me up and dumped me with the Cobbs up in Derby."

"I'm not following. Why don't you start from the beginning?"

"The probation officer came and I was looking at some things from my drawer it's under my bed was under my bed I mean and she grabbed them and took me away without even letting me talk to the father." He was in tears.

She pushed a box of kleenex across the desk without taking her eyes off him.

"So did nobody tell you what was going on? That sounds like a kidnapping. So you've been in this group home up in Derby ever since? That's O.K., take your time."

He told her about the meeting with the assistant district attorney. She nodded as he spoke.

"God, they never told you what this was all about? Unbelievable. That P.O. sounds like a lulu. Let me do a little checking, O.K.? We'll get to the bottom of this."

She was flipping through a rolodex as she spoke. Then on the phone. "Hi, is Albert there?.... Good, I'll wait.... Hi, Albert? Brenda Jenkins here.... O.K., yourself?.... Yep, still the same old.... Listen, know anything about a Father Gregory Morgan, rector at St. Luke's Episcopal in town?.... Oh, I see.... Yeah.... A book of what? Oh my God, that doesn't sound at all like.... O.K., so they dropped the charges.... Yeah.... And where is he now?.... Uh-huh.... Uh-huh.... Hey thanks, and give Min a hug for me, O.K.? Love you guys...." and she put the phone down.

Flannelmouth was huddled up on the chair, silently weeping.

"Flannelmouth, I want you to trust me. I want to help you, O.K.?"

He nodded without looking up.

"There was a book -- and a wristwatch, right?"

He wiped his eyes with the kleenex.

"You said Father Morgan gave them to you, right?"

"Yes." The fiction had virtually become fact in his mind. Middleburg was still too close a reality.

"I'm going to ask you that question again, but before I do I'm going to tell you what has happened to the father. That book you had? That was a book of love poems, As it turns out, that is a book of homosexual poems."

Flannelmouth gasped. "I didn't know," and he started to sob again.

Miss Jenkins went on. "When you said he gave you the book and what it turns out was not just a cheap throwaway watch, they assumed he was behaving inappropriately toward you. Do you know what child molestation is? Are you familiar with the term 'predator?'"

Flannelmouth shook his head.

"It means that adult men -- usually men -- take advantage of children and do bad things to them."

"It was nothing like that. He's a wonderful man."

"I'm sure you're right, but you can see where they might get the wrong idea. They were a little trigger happy in this case, it sounds like, but nevertheless, that's where they went with it. Father Morgan had his enemies in his diocese, apparently. You refused to say anything when the man from the D.A.'s office questioned you, right?"

Flannelmouth nodded.

"That was the end of the criminal investigation, but it wasn't the end of the father's problems. He proved to be an embarrassment to the diocese. He's left the priesthood, probably for good. Nobody's sure what happened to him."

She waited for that to settle in. Then, "Before I ask you that question again, about what happened, I must warn you about something. I am bound by state law to report any cases of criminal conduct I become aware of. You can say nothing and walk away from here and, as far as anybody knows, this conversation never took place."

He didn't wait for her to ask. "I stole them," he wailed.

"O.K. Take your time. O.K., the book we'll forget for the time being. Tell me about the watch. Where did you steal it?"

He was calming down, mopping his eyes with a kleenex. "The Kmart on 14th."

"That's West 14th, right?"

He nodded.

"Do you remember when?"

"I don't know, it was early August I think. Oh, I had to walk around some people on the sidewalk with picket signs. Something about 'nukes' or something like that and something beginning with H."

"Hiroshima by any chance?"

"Yeah, that sounds right."

"OK., I think I know when it was. They'll check with the store. You O.K.?"

He nodded. For some reason, he felt relieved that it was all out in the open. But he couldn't shake the awful feeling about what he'd done to the most important person in his life. And there was no way to undo it.

Miss Jenkins came around the desk and put her arms around him. "You are a very brave boy," she whispered.

Middleburg hadn't changed much since he'd last been there. Except for the director. 'Old Blood and Guts' he was known as. Some said he got the job after he was fired from a private security firm for overzealous enforcement of the rules, and that he wangled his way into Middleburg through some influential friends. It didn't take Flannelmouth long to have a run-in with Mr. Martin, the boss.

It happened during an inspection. Old B. and G., as he was called, started going after a Latino kid named Romero because the boy had forgotten to padlock his footlocker. He was shaking the kid by the shoulder and calling him a 'spic.'

"He forgot," volunteered Flannelmouth.

Old B. and G. let go of Romero and came over to where our young friend stood.

"What's your...oh, Finnegan, is it?"

"Yessir."

"Well, Mr. Finnegan, Tell you what we do with boys who wise off at the director." He turned to the C.O. next to him. "Twenty-four hours in seclusion."

"I didn't wise off, sir."

"Make that forty-eight," and he moved off down the line.

Flannelmouth shrugged as the C.O led him to the seclusion room and opened the heavy steel door. Inside was a padded mat on the floor and a bucket for waste, including the human kind. There was a sink with a single faucet in one corner.

What does a lively young mind do when there's nothing to do? Play brain games. Flannelmouth made up elaborate ways to do multiplication by counting with his fingers. Let's see, if you count by twos, you can do two times anything up to ten. Take off your shoes and you can get all the way up to two times twenty. Same with multiplying by five. Ten was easy. Oh, and eleven; just add the number after you've multiplied by ten. From there he got to multiples of nine: do it by ten and subtract the number. Three: Multiply by two and add the number. Four: Multiply by five and subtract, and so on. It worked fine until he got to seven times eight, but he counted it out and came up with the answer. Quite by accident, he came to the conclusion that multiplication was just a shortcut kind of addition. So if that's true, is division a shortcut kind of subtraction? He was retracing the steps that the ancients trod in creating the basic math functions in the first place.

In like manner, he created dramas about cruel prison wardens and heroic prisoners locked in mortal combat. Needless to say, the prisoners always emerged victorious, often to the cheers of their fellow inmates, but not without a struggle.

Meals were delivered through a slide in the door, so he knew there was a human being out there, but he had no clue beyond that.

Just before lights out, an aide came in to exchange the waste bucket for a new one. It filled the room with the penetrating odor of disinfectant. Then he was alone in the dark. The worst time was night, when the evil spirits descended on him, and the night was filled with snakes, crawly things, angry dogs, and rising waters about to envelop him.

Father Greg is falling into a deep, dark pool. Flannelmouth reaches out to grasp his ankle, and it slips from his grasp. Now he, Flannelmouth, is falling into the pool and sinking below the surface to where there is no light.

He woke up gasping for breath. Nobody to hear him. I could die here, he thought. That ended the sleep for that night.

After breakfast, he was sitting staring at the opposite wall, trying to make faces out of the cracks in the concrete blocks, when he heard somebody fiddling with the key in the lock. The door swung open. He recognized one of the C.O.s.

"Finnegan?"

"Yes."

"Out. Report to the dayroom."

"But I was supposed to be here for 48 hours."

"Guess the boss has a soft spot in his heart."

What Flannelmouth -- and maybe the C.O. -- didn't know was that it had nothing to do with kindly impulses on Old B. and G.'s part but a state law forbidding detention of juveniles in isolation for more than 24 hours. Studies had found that protracted time in isolation could have devastating effects on young minds, leading in some cases to psychotic reactions.

Not that Middleburg always abided by the rule in the cases of its more rebellious spirits. But the infraction had been so minor in this case that keeping Flannelmouth in the room longer would have raised eyebrows even among staff, to say nothing of the impact on the young inmates and the anger that lay just below the surface, waiting only for a trigger to set it off.

What was striking was the speed with which things returned to normal, both for Flannelmouth and those around him. It was almost as if the incident had never happened. Almost. It was one more little insult that would lie in the subconscious, adding to the sense of defeat, helplessness, and hopelessness that pervaded the place.

Things calmed down for Flannelmouth after that. Occasionally a resident (the insiders used the more accurate term, 'inmate') stepped out of line, and the system lashed out. Like so many there, Flannelmouth lived from one day to the next, preoccupied with staying out of trouble and just surviving. He had drawn into a shell, his mind running in circles. He sank into the daily routine of meal time and class time and yard time and bed time, meal time and class time and yard time and bed time.

There were more colored kids now. Some of them were in units formerly reserved for whites. Now there were several colored C.O.s, the result of a court suit challenging the all-white staffing pattern. They were said to be rougher than the white C.O.s, rougher even than Old B. and G. Hard to believe.

Flannelmouth knew the day would come when he'd snap, run afoul of the system in some way. It happened on a Saturday in early October. They were coming in from the yard in the afternoon. Another kid pushed into him, and he pushed back. The wild melee that followed landed four of them in isolation rooms. A few hours later, three were back out in the dayroom watching TV. Flannelmouth remained in isolation. It was generally agreed among staff that he had caused the brawl.

He lay on the mat and drew himself into a ball, wishing there were some way to end it all. There was no more anger in him, just resignation to what would go on and on. Unlike adults, juveniles remained incarcerated 'until rehabilitated.' There were no term limits except adulthood, when they found a new way to hold you or threw you out to the mercy of the streets. That was how many occupants of the Village got there.

Sleep time, with the usual visitations by snakes and snapping dogs and scary people. Wake up time. He was vaguely aware that it was Sunday. Breakfast time. A little later, someone was unlocking the heavy steel door.

"You got company."

Who could that be? Didn't make any sense. The C.O. led him into one of the interview rooms. Seated at the table was Brenda Jenkins, the lady from the county hospital.

"Hi." She waved a hand.

"Hi." He sat down across from her and stared at his hands. The C.O. sat in the corner, stretched, and yawned.

"Well?" she asked.

He shrugged.

"What does that mean?" and she imitated the shrug and cocked her head to one side.

Jesus lady, leave me alone. Another shrug.

"Bad, huh?"

His head was down in his arms. he couldn't stop the tears from coming.

"Listen to me, Flannelmouth, you've got to keep it together. Don't let this place get to you. You got people outside who care about you." She put a hand on his arm.

His head stayed down. He blubbered through the tears, "What are you doing here? Go take care of your patients."

"Hey. The Cobbs asked about you."

"What do they care about a piece of shit?" He finally brought his head up and faced her.

"Oh man." She was talking to the ceiling, and then she bored right in on him.

"Flannelmouth, listen to me. Do not, I say do not let these bastards get to you. They're not worth it. Talk about shit. It's all around you here. Listen, I'm coming back a week from now. You got people in your corner. Do you read me, friend?"

He nodded. She got up, patted his arm, and left.

Once back in isolation with the heavy steel door slammed shut, he pulled the mat over and propped it up against the door. Taking his sweaty boots off, he sat gazing up at the small window to the outside world.

What was that? In the semi-darkness something moved next to the wall. A rat maybe. Very slowly, very carefully, he picked up a boot, then hurled it with all his might at the shadowy figure. It was still there, still moving. Was he hallucinating? He crept closer. A small shoot had forced its way through a crack in the concrete where the wall met the floor, and its tiny leaves trembled at even the slightest movement of air. He thought to himself, it's refusing to die.

Chapter 12.

Connections.

Brenda Jenkins sat in the staff meeting and tuned out the presentation on the new state regs and thought about how she could salvage a frightened, lonely teenager's life. She knew she had no business getting involved with the plight of a kid locked up in that house of horrors, Middleburg. Maybe it was something in the genes, maybe passed down from Grammy Hanks, who bore to her death the head scars from being dragged feet first down the stairs during a sit-in at the Cleveland Board of Ed in the 1960s.

"Brenda." It was her supervisor, Karen Purdy. "You've dealt with a lot of these cases. Do you see any problems?"

God, what is she talking about? "Uh, yeah, well if we have to do it we'll just have to do it. Just seems like we keep getting further away from the patients." She hoped it sounded like she'd been listening. Apparently it did, judging from the nods from a couple other staffers.

"Patient's? What's that? We haven't been able to spend time with patients for the last couple years at least. Except to see who's paying for the service, that is." It was Agnes Flanders. Count on Agnes to tell it like it is. Guts, that Alice. Thank you, Alice.

The eyes off her, Brenda went back to thinking about the kid penned up in Middleburg. Nice kid. Stupid as hell the way he set up the priest he was staying with, but that's fourteen-year-olds. Act first and think about it afterward. Her own kid was a perfect example of that. To say nothing of her own teen years.

The bustle around her told her they were breaking for lunch.

"Lunch?" Agnes was looking at her up close. "Earth to Brenda, earth to Brenda."

"Sorry. I'm a little.... Yeah, bring yours?"

"No, but I'll pick up something downstairs and bring it to your office," and off she went. Good, Brenda needed to talk to somebody about the kid, and Agnes was the right person for it.

A short while later they sat across from each other at the small conference table in Brenda's office.

"He giving you trouble? You sure looked like something was bugging you this morning."

"No, all quiet on the Ralph front. It's about a kid in Middleburg."

Agnes was busy managing her tuna sandwich. She finally got out, "Middleburg? I thought the state closed them down a year ago."

"No such luck. Anyway, there's a kid who's getting destroyed by that outfit, and I'm trying to figure a way to get him out."

Agnes mulled it over. "How'd you get into that one? Dosn't exactly sound like medical."

"It isn't. Well, that's the way I got into it, but.... It's complicated."

"Sounds complicated. So what's it all about?

Brenda put down her sandwich. It was easier with two hands. "This kid's father was in here -- classic cirrosis of the liver, plus he had diabetes."

"...and a little drinking problem."

"That, too. Anyway, he eventually died."

"Score one for County Memorial," said Agnes,

"That's how I got to know the son, a fourteen-year-old. Anyway, the kid told me he'd stolen something -- an expensive watch, it turned out. I warned him beforehand about the reporting reqirement, but he told me anyway."

"So you helped land him in Middleburg."

Brenda nodded with a wry expression.

"God, Brenda, are you off on one of your save-the-world expeditions?"

"Just one occupant of it."

"Hmm. Anything for NAACP to grab onto? They've got a sharp young lawyer on their regional staff now who specializes...."

"The kid is white."

"White?"

"Yep. Irish white."

"I hate to say it," said Agnes, "but that may make it easier."

"So any other ideas? I really don't know where to begin on this one. I'm concerned about the kid's holding it together. He keeps landing in isolation, which is not exactly a great thing for one's mental state. He also has a history of running, so they keep him very restricted. I wouldn't be surprised if they were keeping him on meds to make it easier to handle him. You know what that place is like."

"Any family? Family friends? Agencies involved?"

"Nobody."

"...Except Brenda Jenkins."

The other nodded. 'Yep, you got it in a nutshell."

Agnes munched on the remains of her sandwich in silence. She glanced at her watch. "Uh-oh, we're overdue in the meeting."

They tossed their trash in the basket and headed back to the conference room.

A few miles away at that moment, Flannelmouth Finnegan was sitting at a picnic table in the day room at Middleburg, playing the umpteenth game of solitaire and ignoring the buzz around him. A hand reached out from across the table and scooped up the cards.

"Hey, what the shit do you think...."

The Spanish kid Romero held the pack up with one hand and waved the index finger of the other. As Flannelmouth watched, the kid fanned out the cards face down on the table.

"Pick one," he said.

Flannelmouth, eager for anything to break up the boredom, pulled a card toward him.

"Look at the card," said Romero. It was the queen of hearts. "No, don't show me or nothin'," as he pushed the rest of the deck together. He lifted half the deck and said, "put the card there," motioning to the rest of the deck on the table.

Flannelmouth did as he was told, and Romero put the other half on top. He riffed the cards a couple of times, then cut the deck again. "Look at the top card," he instructed, nodding to the stack of cards on the table.

It was the four of diamonds.

"Hah, I got ya," said Flannelmouth triumphantly.

"Yeah, so you did," said the other, tossing the queen of hearts in front of him.

"How'd you do that?"

Romero shrugged with a little smile. He glanced around to see where the C.O. was sitting and said, "Thanks."

"Oh yeah, you mean that time Old B. and G. was coming down on you. I just don't like to see them screwing over anybody. That's the way this whole craphouse operates," and he nodded at the dead TV screen on the wall, mass punishment for a minor infraction of the rules by 'some one of you guys.'

"What they got you in here for?" asked Romero.

"I stole something. How about you?"

"Drugs. I was doin' lookout mainly. South Side, you know."

"I thought that was the blacks."

"Oh, yeah, that was part of the problem. Lots of turf fights between the Spanish and the blacks. We each had our territory, but the lines kept changin'. These two black cops was out to nail us. Somebody said they was gettin' paid off by somebody on the other side. So I got picked up in a raid, and so here I am."

He picked up the cards. "You with a gang?"

"No, man, just by myself. Been that way from the beginning."

"Cool," said Romero, "the Lone Ranger."

Not so cool, thought Flannelmouth. He was wondering if Ms. Jenkins would come back, or would she drop him the way so many had in the past?

Romero turned the cards face up on the table, then pulled out the four jacks and a queen. "You see, there was these four princes went off to seek their fortune." He turned each card over.

Flannelmouth watched closely, determined not to be fooled again.

"Their mother, the queen, wondered if she'd ever see them again." Romero pulled the rest of the deck together, flipped it over, tucked the queen in somewhere in the middle, placed one jack on top, one jack on the bottom, and the other two in the middle of the deck somewhere. He riffed the deck, cut it a couple of times, then rapped on top three times.

"Here," he said, handing the cards to Flannelmouth, "Let's see if the three princes got home."

Flannelmouth turned the cards face up and went through them. The queen and the four jacks sat together midway through the deck.

"Ta-da," said Romero.

Flannelmouth was thinking about the whole concept of getting home. Such a familiar part of life to most of us, it was something of an abstraction for the lad. He wondered what the father was doing just then.

*

Greg Morgan stood ladling soup into plastic cups in the Sisters of St Francis dining room, as hungry eyes watched from just outside the door.

"Just a few more minutes, guys," he said.

Sister Jennifer checked the coffee urn and went back to putting out the rolls and cupcakes. "Let's see, O.K., napkins, soup spoons. O.K., let them in."

The customers lined up and waited for Greg to bless the food. He was sure God didn't care whether he was a priest or a layman. The sisters seemed not to.

"Thank you, God, for bringing us together this day to enjoy your bountiful harvest. And bless those who cannot be with us this day." A few amens from the assemblage. "We thank you, God, for bestowing on us this food when so many go without, and there is much hunger in the land and in the world." More amens. "Lord bless this food to our use and us to Thy service, and make us ever mindful of the needs of others. In Jesus's name, Amen."

Amens throughout the group. Sister Jennifer crossed herself, as did several others in the room.

The diners knew the routine and kept to it like well-trained soldiers. Each in turn came by the serving table to take a spoon and a napkin, hold them together in one hand with the cup of soup, place the roll and the cupcake on top, then nod or not to toward the milk pitcher, wait for the coffee to be poured and take that in the free hand. It was a balancing act that would have done an experienced juggler proud.

As the diners -- mostly men, with a few women, some with children -- ate, Greg and Sister Jennifer started to pull things together. They would wait another twenty minutes for the stragglers, but folks knew if they tarried too long there would be no food that day.

Last to eat were Greg and Sister Jennifer. Sister Patrice Ann came down to join them. Once or twice he had suggested sitting and eating with the diners, breaking bread together as it were, but the sisters had their system and weren't looking to change it.

As the three of them sat eating, Sister Patrice asked, "Ever hear anything from the young man?"

"You mean Flannelmouth?"

She nodded. They'd had more than a few sessions, with the sister helping Greg get out his rage.

"I think about him a lot, sister." He put down the roll. "I'm learning how hard it is to forgive. I used to counsel people on that all the time. Boy, different thing when it's you that's supposed to do the forgiving."

"How well I know," said Sister Patrice Ann. "During the war in El Salvador, we had refugees who had been through unspeakable acts of cruelty. Forced to watch family members slaughtered, daughters raped. What amazed me was the way they were able to forgive their tormentors, put that behind them, and move on."

"Some people say 'never forget,'" said Greg.

"Oh I know. And it's important not to forget -- both the perpetrator and his victim. But it was so liberating for those people to be able to forgive. Hate can be such a terrible burden to carry around with you."

For the rest of the day, Greg thought about their conversation. He wondered what had happened to Flannelmouth. All he knew was that the youth had confessed to stealing the incriminating objects, too late to reverse Greg's decision to leave the priesthood, or to salvage the engagement to Pamela. He supposed the kid had been sent back to Middleburg. So, the hell with him, Greg was ready to move on with his life, Now he had to think about that a little more. Think about. The forgiving would take time.

Chapter 13.

Laps.

It all started when seven boys were caught smoking pot in the boiler room of Building One. Flannelmouth wasn't one of them. He was steering clear of anything that could give them an excuse to throw him in isolation 'and throw the key away,' as he put it. His friend Romero was part of the group, however, and with his history, suspicion immediately focused on him.

There were endless grilling sessions in the room next to Old B. and G.'s office, some lasting into the A.M. hours. Who brought in the pot? That was the question they kept hammering away at. Romero denied it and nobody else was talking.

The decision to order the whole lot of them out to do laps around the big field at the rear of the property 'until you drop' was vintage B. and G.: impulsive and mean-spirited. And once he gave the order, it would not be revisited.

Everybody was ordered out to watch the show. Truth to tell, they didn't need much urging. Unusually warm for October. Fine day for a run, everybody agreed.

As the seven took off, two black kids sprinted on ahead of the rest, to the cheers of the crowd. Romero trailed the other four as they finished the first lap. He shot a very unhappy look at Flannelmouth as he went by. Flannelmouth didn't like the feel of the whole operation, but he cheered along with the rest.

Second lap, and some of them began falling back. A tubby kid named Orville Damon was barely going through the motions. The crowd egged him on. "Come on, Orville, great way to lose weight," yelled a kid as he went by.

When Romero came around a second time, Flannelmouth called out to him, "Pace yourself," but he shook off the advice and plowed on.

Fourth lap. The first to go down was Orville. He stumbled once, caught himself, then stumbled again and landed in a heap by the side of the 'track' that was marked by penants fluttering from thin stakes at the inside corners. Gasping for breath, he slowly got up and hobbled back to the starting place. He was greeted by a healthy round of boos from the crowd.

Flannelmouth lost count. It had to be seven or eight laps at least.

A kid Flannelmouth didn't know was next. He went down and stayed down. Two of the C.O.s went over to make sure he was O.K. Meanwhile, the two black kids were running as if they were just starting the marathon. Far behind, Romero kept gamely on, going slower and slower. On the back stretch he went down and lay still. Flannelmouth ran across to where he lay and was looking down at his friend as the C.O.s came up.

"Get away from him," one snarled, and Flannelmouth backed away.

The other C.O. was suddenly standing up and yelling, "Somebody call 9-1-1."

Ignored in the panic that followed, Flannelmouth went over and looked down into Romeros face. It was a funny color, and there was no motion. He reached down and grabbed the wrist. No pulse that he could feel. Maybe just the commotion around him. But he knew better. The kid was dead.

Brenda Jenkins looked down from her office window and watched an ambulance back into one of the docks, as she picked up the phone, tapped in a number, and waited.

"Hi, this is Brenda Jenkins, County Memorial Social Service.... Yes, I wonder if John Mallon is around.... Yes, I'll wait.... Hi, John.... Same to you, dear. Hey, got a problem.... Yeah, I know, that's what I get paid for, right? You know that thing about Middleburg training school the senator was investigating a year ago?.... Yes, that's the one.... Well I know he did. That's why I'm calling you. Listen, there's a kid out there I'm really concerned about. Decent kid who made some foolish decisions, and.... Yes, I know. If they could only just skip over adolescence. But you know I don't call the senator unless it's serious.... Right, that would be fine. Just a mini scandal? I'll try to cook one up. Meanwhile, I'd love to be able to get this kid out of there.... I know, as long as they're licensed, the county doesn't.... Yeah. Here's the problem. They keep throwing him in isolation for nothing....Oh, yes, do I ever? One kid burned to death while they fiddled around looking for the keys.... No, he's been getting depressed lately, and of course their idea of treatment for depression is to strap them down and give them a shot of electricity. When does that go back to, the early fifties? Anyway, see what you can do, O.K.?"

She sat hitting the phone against the desk until the voice came on with, "If you'd like to make a call...."

Midmorning and Brenda was out on a home visit. On her way back to the office she was wracking her brains, trying to come up with something. She kept trying to think of people who could help. There was the priest, of course -- ex-priest, that is. Even if she could locate him, he'd probably be in no mood to do any favors for the kid who ruined his life. The Cobbs? They were concerned, but they knew less about the kid than she did. What about the nuns that run that mission on Seventh Street?

Somebody had mentioned them a few times. The priest was it? Or maybe Flannelmouth, She wasn't sure. What the hell? Worth a try.

Sister Jennifer took the the call.

"Hi, my name is Brenda Jenkins, I'm with Social Service at County Memorial."

"Yes, Ms. Jenkins, we know of the fine work your people do. How may I help you?"

"I believe you knew a Seamus Finnegan."

"Oh yes indeed. A wonderful man. He is so missed. We had the funeral for him here at Sisters of St. Francis."

Weird. Oh well, why not?

"It was the wish if his son," said Sister Jennifer.

"You mean Flannel...Vernal?"

Sister Jennifer laughed. "Flannelmouth," and she laughed again. "Delightful boy. I hope he's all right."

"As a matter of fact, I'm calling about the son. I'm wondering if you have any idea what's become of the Episcopal priest he was staying with. Morgan was the name. He was rector at St. Luke's over near West 14th Street."

"Yes, wait just a minute, I'll check to see if he's in."

In? It took Brenda a few seconds to process that one.

"You mean he's with you?" She was wondering if the guy had just switched venues. Hell, keep the collar and just start saying mass.

"Yes, Greg has been a great help. He and I run the soup kitchen, and he also helps the children with their homework. We're hoping he'll help us open up our gym and have something for the older boys. Wait a moment, and I'll see if he's here."

Unbelievable. The old guy upstairs works in mysterious ways, his wonders to perform.

"Hello."

"Hello, Greg Morgan?"

"Yes. Is this Ms. Jenkins?"

"I think I fell off the bus somewhere along the way. You're the last person I expected to be talking to."

He laughed. "Life is full of surprises, no?"

"Yeah, you bet. Listen, I want to get together with you. It's about Flannemouth."

"Is he O.K.?" It came very fast. Obviously concerned about the kid.

"Yes and no. I need to talk with you."

"Uh-huh. As you can imagine, I'm still dealing with a few things."

"Absolutely. I do understand." She waited. Don't make him feel pressured.

"What did you have in mind?"

Good. We're over that hurdle, she thought. "Any chance of coming out to my office?"

"That's a little problem. I don't have a car. Besides, I'm sort of committed here at St. Francis during the day."

"O.K. No problema. Stay right there. I'll come by and pick you up. Let's see, how about 6:30? You do eat dinner, I assume."

"Well, I...uh...well, O.K."

*

Flannelmouth was devastated by the turn of events, of course. In fact, a pall hung over every part of Middleburg. Meanwhile, the upper echelons went into crisis mode. There was a scramble to destroy any records that might cause a problem. Like the medical records indicating a possible heart condition and the fact that Romero had complained about breathing problems a number of times without any visible response from the organization.

Old B. and G. put out the word: Any communication with anybody outside would be cleared with the office. There would be a C.O. present at all family visits, That meant, of course, a sharp decline in family visits on weekends, since they had fewer C.O.'s on duty then.

Flannelmouth sat in the dayroom staring into space. One of the older guys sat down next to him. Flannelmouth knew him only as Buddy.

"Bad, what happened to Romero there."

"Yeah." Flannelmouth couldn't manage any more than that.

"They expect state people to be all over this place. That's why the lockdown."

"He showed me card tricks. The guy was a genius."

Buddy moved a little closer, picked a magazine off the table, and started thumbing through it. "Know anybody on the outside?"

Flannelmouth knew enough not to look at him. "I don't know, why?"

"I got something I want to get out of here. It's dynamite. I know you've had your problems with the management."

"Uh-uh, Buddy, I don't think so." Flannelmouth was thinking about the wristwatch and the book of poems. All he'd need would be to have them find something in his room.

"You know what the official line is? The boys were just having a race. Nothing about the punishment."

Flannelmouth pricked up his ears. He checked out the C.O. sitting in the corner, staring out the window. "So what you got?"

Buddy stuck his hand in his breast pocket and brought it out, apparently empty. Then, down below the level of the tabletop, he opened it to reveal what looked like a small cell phone. "I got Old B. and G. on here telling the guys they're going to run till they drop."

"Shake," said Flannelmouth, and he extended his hand. When he took it away he had the device.

Buddy moved off and went to check out the action at the pool table. Flannelmouth went back to staring into space, his mind full of Seamus in the hospital and Mr. Rat so peaceful in the trap and Romero lying there on the ground.

As Brenda was driving to the Sisters of St. Francis, she turned on the radio to check the latest traffic. Still rush hour. She wanted to get there before Greg had a change of mind. Her mind was elsewhere when the local news came on. "...died this afternoon...juvenile correctional...Middleburg...."

Oh my God, she thought, he didn't. She pulled off to the side, brought the car to a stop, and put on her flashers. Her hands were shaking as she turned up the volume. No, some kid named Romero. She let out a long sigh.

Greg was standing in front of the mission. He looked older and thinner. Hadn't been that long since she'd last seen him. Maybe it was the sweatshirt and no clerical collar. She lowered the window as she drew up alongside him. "Hi. Know any good places to eat around here?"

"There's a Chinese restaurant the next street over. Pizza joint a little further down on 7th."

"O.K. Chinese is good. Can I park here?"

"Yes. Just don't park overnight, or you may have to get it out of the city garage for a bundle. I think it's one-fifty or some ridiculous sum."

She pulled over closer to the curb, flipped the locks, and came around to where he stood. Shake or hug? Hell, hugs are good, and she put her arms out. Yes, good hug.

Things were closing down in the neigborhood. Metal doors were coming down to clang shut. Greg led her around the corner to the little Chinese restaurant with the blinking red sign. Inside, the man at the desk nodded to the empty seats. "Any place O.K."

Once they'd placed their orders, she settled back a little.

"You live around here?"

"It's a short walk from here."

"It's so neat, you working with the sisters."

"It's been a lifesaver in more ways than one." He cocked his head to one side and brought his eyes up to meet hers. "So, you wanted to talk."

"Yep. I think I have a pretty good picture of what happened."

"You mean with Flannelmouth? That's pretty simple. Kid stole a bunch of stuff, made up a cock and bull story to save his hide, and here I am. And to think I trusted the kid."

"Greg, you have a right to be mad as hell. But I wonder if you know the whole story."

The food came, and that sort of took over the conversation for while.

"Like what?"

"Like what what?"

"So what's the whole story?"

"Oh, right. O.K. First of all, he had no idea what that book of poems was. The P.O. walked in on him and demanded to make a search. She didn't tell him anything about the child molestation business, wouldn't let him talk to you. It was like vigilantes from the old west."

"That isn't what they said. They told me he was afraid of me and wanted to be taken out of there."

"Totally false. He kept asking to see you, and they refused. You know about his meeting with the assistant D.A.?"

"No, I don't know about any meeting. All I knew was they got the kid to confess. Seems he stole the things."

"In the first place, *they* didn't get him to confess, I did. Or rather he volunteered the information when he found out what had happened to you, even though he knew it would probably land him back in Middleburg. He was devastated. You're still primo uno with him."

Greg sat dumfounded.

"About the meeting with the D.A.'s staff, they questioned him, assuming he would help them nail you. Instead, he said nothing, single-handedly killing the criminal case. They had him in a group home up in Derby -- under close watch so he wouldn't run."

"I knew he refused to cooperate, but never heard any of the rest of it."

"Tell me, reverend, did you ever hurt somebody you really cared about and not been able to undo it?"

He sat gazing at the bowl of white rice neither one of them had touched. "Yes, of course. In seminary, I let my roommate take the fall for something I had done. Didn't have the guts to come forward. Worried it would hurt my stupid career. It practically ended his."

"Forgiving's not easy. It's taken me...." No, don't bring that up. Too close to the bone.

"What?"

O.K., why not? "I had a rough time in my marriage. That's all in the past now. Took a while to get all that behind me."

"You have children?" Good. Safer territory.

"One. Tara's just twenty. Heading off for college soon. Already talking about going into law eventually. I was too young when she came along. Had to drop out of high school. Finished by getting my G.E.D.

The food came and attention shifted to that. As they ate, Brenda said, "How about you? What's her name, Pamela?"

"Oh that," and he laughed.

"Did I say something funny?"

"Oh, no. It's just that when all that stuff came out, and the diocese decided I was an embarrassment, Pam sort of lost interest in the relationship. She decided I wasn't the guy for her. Truth to tell, I wasn't."

"That kid loves you. Right now he's being destroyed by that place, which is why I needed to talk to you."

"Thanks. I'm glad you did. God, all kinds of ways to hurt people, aren't there?" He was silent for a moment, then, "About Flannelmouth, he used to tell me about nightmares he was having."

"Nightmares?"

"Nightmares. From the sound of it, they came right out of the rich lore of Irish mythology, which I studied in college for some dumb reason. I assume he was getting this from his father, you know, stories from the old country. Seamus was like that."

It took Greg a minute to get back on course. "Anyway, so what do you suggest?"

"I'm trying to figure a way to get him out of there. I've been in touch with the state senator's office. He owes me one. He tried to get Middleburg closed down last year."

"I should get out to see Flannelmouth."

"That may be a problem for now. I was just hearing on the radio that a kid died there today. I'm sure there'll be an investigation, which means it will be off limits for while."

"Any idea what happened?"

"My bet is it has to do with the medical care, or lack of it. That place is notorious for hiring idiots with political connections to run their health service."

"Maybe your friend the senator will get his wish after all."

"Doubt it. They've managed to wiggle out of every situation up to now."

As they walked back to her car, Greg said, "So how come you're so involved with this case? Isn't it a little out of your line?"

She took a minute to answer. "I hate to see kids, anybody, messed over by that system. That's how I got into this line of work in the first place. I just never was good at setting boundaries around what I do."

He knew exactly what she was talking about.

The next day's papers and TV news reported on an unfortunate incident at the Middleburg Juvenile Training Center. A spirited race first proposed by the residents had ended in tragedy when one of the contestants died in the middle of the run. A tearful B. and G. spoke of how the whole community had been brought together by the death. The state would be conducting a routine investigation.

About midmorning, Brenda got a call from Senator McFadden's office.

It was John Mallon's voice. "See this morning's paper?"

"Sure. It's been all over the TV. I heard it on the radio last night."

"Romero's mother is saying he had a heart condition. For some reason the school is having a hard time finding his medical records."

"Check with the county health department. They keep good records. That stuff should all be in their computer. I'll check to see if we have anything here at County Memorial. Of course, who knows whether Middleburg ever reports anything?"

They agreed to compare notes later in the day.

*

Everything was on hold at Middleburg. Flannelmouth carefully wrapped the cell phone in his handkerchief and tucked it inside his underpants. He pressed it down as flat as he could. A slight bulge, but not really noticeable. One place they never patted you down was your crotch, front and center.

Calling on old instincts, he watched the comings and goings of the trucks. Garbage pick up at 6:30 A.M. Only the driver was on that detail. Bakery truck at ten. Other provisions came in the afternoon, between three and four. Mail delivery late afternoon, sometimes not until five. He settled on the garbage truck. It made its rounds, starting at the headquarters and security building and ending at Building Three, well out of sight of the rest of the complex.

The next Tuesday night, Flannelmouth complained to the C.O. about stomach cramps.

Predictably, the guy showed little interest and said he should report to the dispensary the next morning. Flannelmouth made several trips to the bathroom that night, each time locking the stall door behind him and flushing the toilet a few times.

Early the next morning, he checked to see if anybody was awake. Not a sign of life down the line. He got up, dressed, and carried his pajamas and shower shoes to the bathroom and into the last stall. He locked the door, positioned the shower shoes to look as if his feet were in them, then slid out of the narrow opening at the bottom. He hoped people would assume he was sitting on the john. If he was missing at breahfast, it would figure; he had made sure everybody knew his somach was upset. Anything to buy a little time.

Keeping to the wooded area away from the main roadway though the complex, he ran to Building Three and hid behind the utility shed, then waited until the truck pulled up next to the garbage cans. The driver emptied them into the back of the truck, then hopped into the cab and headed for the main gate, unaware that he had a passenger in back.

Flannelmouth burrowed down into the garbage, fighting the impulse to puke. The C.O. on duty yawned, took a quick glance into the truck, and waved the driver on. Only after he figured he was a good ways away from the hated place did our young friend come up for air.

Chapter 14.

The good guys win for a change.

The truck rode on for what seemed like a hundred miles and finally came to a halt and sat still. No traffic light this. No cars whipping by on the other side. Cautiously, Flannelmouth edged up so he could see past the top of the cab. They were at the entrance to the city dump. The truck he was in was third in line. He could see the driver below, talking with a man in a little shed and handing papers to him. Perfect. Just climb out and away we go.

By now a couple of trucks had pulled up behind them. Flannelmouth waved to the next driver as he climbed over the edge of the truck and hopped down. What he failed to notice was a police car sitting just across the way.

"Stop that kid," somebody yelled. It was none other than the driver of the truck from which our friend had just alit. "He's on the run."

Before he knew it, Flannelmouth was being grabbed from behind by a police officer. Then came an amazing transformation. Down on the ground he went, eyes wide with terror, grabbing at his throat.

"What is it kid?" asked the cop.

Flannelmouth struggled to speak, but the words wouldn't come. Finally, "asthma.... In my left pocket.... inhalator."

The cop reached down and felt around. "Nothing here, kid."

"Oh God... must have left them.... Emergency room...please."

A few minutes later, Flannelmouth was sitting in the back of a police cruiser, racing toward County Memorial Hospital with its siren blaring at the intersections. Bumpy ride. At least they could provide seat cushions, he thought.

The cruiser drove up to the emergency entrance. The officer came around and opened the door. "Are you O.K., son?"

"I think so, sir.... Thanks...."

"Need a stretcher?"

"No...sir.... I think...I can make it."

"Here, son, put your arm over my shoulder.... That's right...easy now."

A man in whites came around to his other side, and together they got him to a gurney and heisted him onto it. The nurse or whatever was preparing a hypodermic needle.

Flannelmouth waved it off. "I'm on...some medications. Call...Ms. Jenkins...Social Service...she knows...what I'm on."

The man in whites motioned to an aide who had come up to help. The latter was soon on a cell phone. "Yes, this is the E.R. Is Ms. Jenkins there? There's a young man here asking for her.... Yes, I'll wait." Then he turned to Flannelmouth. What's your name?"

"Finne...Finnegan."

Then into the cell phone, "Yes, Ms. Jenkins, there's a kid down here, came in with an asthma attack.... Finnegan, ma'am.... He says you know him.... Yes, I'll put him on."

He held the phone up to Flannelmouth's ear.

"Flannelmouth, is that you?"

"Yes."

"Listen, I'll be right down."

The nurse put a thermometer under Flannelmouth's tongue and wrapped a blood pressure cuff around his upper arm. In a minute, "Temperature 99.1, blood pressure elevated a little but within normal range. You feeling a little better, son?"

Flannelmouth nodded. "Thank you, sir. I'm doing better. These things come and go, you know."

The cop stepped forward. "Middleburg?"

Flannelmouth nodded.

"O.K., as soon as you can travel, I'll get you back there. Let them deal with this."

Just then Ms. Jenkins appeared above the youth, a worried expression on her face. He motioned to her to come closer. "I've got something for you," he whispered, reaching down inside his underpants and pulling out the handkerchief. "Here, inside," and he handed it to her.

She nodded. "Take care of yourself," and she gave him a little pat on the cheek. "We'll be in touch."

A while later Brenda watched as he slid off the gurney and was led to the waiting police car.

Back in her office, she studied the device Flannelmouth had handed to her. "Hey," she said to a passing secretary, "know what this is?"

"Cell phone. You do know cell phones, don't you, Brenda,?" Our Ms. Jenkins was not known around the office for her digital know-how.

"Don't be smart, Jen. Of course I know what a cell pbone is. But I'm thinking this one can do other things besides make phone calls."

"Wouldn't be knowing. Better get Darrell - he's the expert around here."

For an hour, in between job-related tasks, she fooled with the buttons on the front of the phone. Envelope? She pushed the tiny icon that looked like the back of an envelope. A grainy image appeared on the screen. There was a voice that sounded even more grainy. Impossible to make out what was being said, but she knew it must be important.

Brenda spotted Darrell going by. "Hey, old friend, got a minute?"

"For you, my dear, I'd *make* the time. Whassup?"

She showed him the grainy image.

"Nice piece of goods. That cost somebody a piece of change. Audio and video, too."

"But I can't make out what I'm looking at."

"Plug it into your computer."

"Plug it into my computer. Plug into my computer. Er...."

"Right here on the side. Let's see, you should have a port on the side of the phone - yeah, right there. Got a USB?"

"USB...USB...," said Brenda.

"Connector," said the expert. "Hmm, that's going to take a small one. I don't happen to have one. Go to Radio Shack. They can fix you up."

"O.K., got to make sure I've got this right." She was jotting things down on a pad.

"Show them the phone and they'll figure it out. Brenda, you ought to get with the 21st century, you know?"

Smart ass, she thought. "O.K., thanks for the time and the advice, dear." She turned off the phone and dropped it into her purse.

That night when Tara got home, Brenda asked her about a -- lessee, as she flipped open the pad...lessee here, O.K. -- "USB."

"You got one in the drawer there next to the computer."

Brenda showed her the cell phone.

"Oh," said the other, "that's going to take something smaller. I think I have one in my room."

Tara went and soon returned waiving the USB in the air. She opened the small cover on the side of the cell phone and, "There, yeah, got it. Now, see on the side of your computer? Put the other end in there."

Brenda did as she was told. Nice, in a way, to have your daughter showing you the ropes, instead of the other way around. There's hope for the future, she thought.

"Nothing's happening."

"Yes there is. Look, that icon at the top of your screen."

Benda gave it a couple of taps, and in a moment the screen was filled by a frozen image with a play button in the middle. It was a man talking to a group of some kind.

She activated the video. "O.K., nobody's talking? All right, this afternoon, you seven right here will engage in a little recreational activity known as 'run till you drop.' We used to do that in the Marines. Make a man out of you. And everybody else will be in the audience."

Question from someone in the audience, inaudible. "No, screw that, I said everybody." As the man swung his gaze in the direction of whoever was doing the recording, the image went black.

Brenda knew exactly what she was looking at. "My God," she said, "he's condemning that kid Romero to death."

"Huh?" Tara looked puzzled.

"It's O.K.," said her mother, "You may be watching history in the making."

The next morning, as soon as Brenda got to the office, she picked up the phone and punched in a number.

"John Mallon, please.... Brenda Jenkins. He knows me.... I see, when is he expected? As soon as he comes in, please ask him to call me... yes, at my office at County Memorial. Tell him it's urgent..... Matter of life and death? You might say that.... Yes, I'll wait."

Brenda fussed around her office for what seemed like hours until John's call came.

"Hi, Brenda, sorry we're pretty...."

"Hi, John. Listen, I have a video recording that is going to blow you away.... That race when the kid at Middleburg died? That was no activity the kids thought up. The boss man ordered it, some kind of punishment apparently.... Exactly.... Never mind how I got hold of it. I'm sure it's the genuine article.... O.K., I'll hang until you get back to me."

She replayed the passage a few more times to make sure she was hearing it right. No question. It came through clear as a bell. That recorder must be top quality goods. No doubt stolen by one of the inmates. No matter. This could be the end of that regime out there. No, she knew it didn't work that way. At best they'd lop off the head of the head man and go right back to doing their Middleburg thing. All of which made the mission even clearer: Get Flannelmouth out of there.

The phone rang. "Yes, this is Brenda Jenkins.... Oh, Senator McFadden, how are you?.... Yes, been a few years. That campaign in.... Well, thank you. We do what we can.... O.K., John filled you in?.... That's right.... No, first of all, it picked up everything very clearly. I don't know the man personally, but.... A C.O.? Yes, could be. It will be easy enough to know who it is when somebody else looks at it.... Oh, of course, let me check my calendar.... This Friday?.... O.K., yes, that will work. I'll reserve the conference room. Should be free then. Friday afternoon they clear out of here pretty fast.... Oh, while I have you on the line, there's a boy up there that I'm really concerned about. Name of Vernal Finnegan.... That's right, V-E-R.... Right.... Oh, that would be great.... Yes, it sure would, especially coming from you, senator...."

Brenda sank back in her chair with a big smile. For once, things were moving in the right direction.

*

Flannelmouth was in an especially cheerful mood as he was returned to a seclusion room. As he was led through the day room, he waved to the guys sitting around, and they gave him a round of applause. Buddy was studying the cover of a magazine and didn't look up.

He'd delivered the goods to Ms. Jenkins. Now he could tolerate anything they threw at him. And throw they did. As soon as the 24 hours were up, and he was back in the dayroom, the mess hall, or the barracks, C.O.s would deliberately provoke him. When they took him back for another bout of isolation, he shrugged.

Then all at once, for no apparent reason, they were leaving him alone. The other guys noticed. Maybe he'd agreed to be the house rat. There were all kinds of rumors about guys who, it was said, were spies for the management.

"You ratting, Finnegan?" It was one of the old heads from Building Two.

"No way, man."

"Then why the kid gloves treatment all of a sudden?" asked another.

"Beats me."

"You stayed out of that little pot party in the boiler room that time. How come?" The speaker was pressing up against him. Flannelmouth fought the urge to hit him or even push back.

"Leave the guy alone." It was Buddy. The others backed off after that. But from then on, the rest of the guys avoided Flannelmouth and left him out of their conversations. Worse in some ways than the isolation rooms.

The fact was, the atmosphere had changed for everybody. For whatever reason, the sheer brutality was less evident. Trips to isolation were becoming increasingly rare. What Flannelmouth and the others couldn't know was that a phone call from the office of State Senator Ted McFadden had triggered the change. Old B. and G. knew something was in the air. But having successfully weathered the initial reaction to Romero's death. he assumed he was in the clear. Besides, he had connections. But no point in taking chances, so things eased up at Middleburg.

*

Brenda made sure the coffee and hot water carafes and the usual setup were in place on the side table of the conference room. She had her secretary, Judy, on alert in case they needed anything. This was the senator's meeting, so she'd leave the conference table bare except for her laptop, a legal pad, and a couple of pens next to it.

At 2:45, John Mallon came in, cousin-kissed Brenda, and looked at his watch. "The senator should be here any minute. He had a meeting downtown. Where's the...?"

Brenda pointed at the device next to the computer.

"Good," said John, "we're anxious to see it."

At 3:05, Judy, the secretary, brought Senator McFadden in. Sixty something, immaculately dressed, the senator had a carefully coiffed bush of white hair. He was followed by a man Brenda didn't recognize. She nodded to Judy, who left the room, closing the door behind her. The senator shook hands with Brenda and then gestured toward the other man. "This is Bill Rosen. He handles our legal business. Bill worked on the Middleburg case before."

They shook hands.

"Coffee or tea anybody? Help yourselves," she said, going to the side table. "Senator?"

"No, thank you just the same."

They were soon settled around the table.

"Well, young lady," said the senator, "John says you may have some interesting information about our friend Luther Martin."

John nodded in the direction of the laptop. Brenda swung it around so it faced the senator, tapped the computer into life, waited till the icon appeared, and opened it revealing the now-familiar image.

"That's him," said John. Bill Rosen came around behind the senator to watch. Brenda hit the play button, and the now familiar tirade unwound.

Bill Rosen whispered something to the senator, who nodded.

"Nice guy," said John.

When people were settled down, the senator spoke.

"O.K., here's where we are. Let me deal with Mr. Martin first. He needs to get out of there, that's obvious. Aside from ordering the Romero boy out on what amounted to a death march, there's a whole history of neglect regarding his heart condition. Bill tells me the best we can get on him is manslaughter, maybe three to five years. They will plead ignorance about the condition. But I want us to look at the bigger picture.

"Middleburg has been a problem for years. Should have been shut down a decade ago. Thought we had them for good a year ago when we went after them. This goes way beyond Luther, who has only been in charge for a few years. So it's not just Luther who looks bad but the whole organization, the board, everybody. That board has ignored the situation for years. So what

I'm thinking is we use this incident to lever a real change in the place."

"Like shutting it down?" asked Brenda.

"Never happen," said the senator. "I found that out last year. There are some powerful people in this state who think we're already too lenient with what they consider animals. In their eyes, Middleburg is the shining example of how to treat young criminals.

"No, I think we can use this incident to force a total overhaul of the place. It's happened before. Anybody acquainted with Tanner Farms?"

"They do a wonderful job with their girls," said Brenda. They've won some awards with my professional association."

"Well -- and Bill here will back me up on this -- there was a time when they were twice as bad as Middleburg -- with girls, yet. It was the rape of one of their residents by a staff member that set off a big investigation. That's why it's a different place now.

"We convict our friend Luther of manslaughter, and they'll just replace him. If instead we hold that over their heads, we may just be able to turn that place into something decent. The last thing that place needs is a scandal over that kid's death. It would affect their ability to raise money, get referrals, everything. If we just sit some of those board people down in private and show them that video...."

Bill Rosen whispered to him.

"Yes, Bill says it sounds too much like blackmail. O.K., we pose the issue. If they say they want to see evidence, well...."

"Does that mean Mr. Martin will go free?" Brenda asked.

"In a way, that may be the price we pay for getting Middleburg overhauled. We'll get him out of the place -- and we can make sure he never works in juvenile corrections again, or any corrections, for that matter, at least in this state. But we hear the family will bring a civil suit regardless."

To Brenda it sounded like a sellout, but she saw no choice: Without the senator involved, the whole case might go nowhere. As it was, Middleburg would probably come back to haunt him in the next election.

Senator McFadden went on. "Brenda, I'm going to need your help on this. You can help us find a team to come in and blueprint the overhaul."

Well, the guy knew how to use flattery, that was for sure.

"I can start checking around," she said, "I have contacts back at school who know the juvenile corrections field. They'll know who's doing consulting."

"Oh, by the way," said the senator, "how did you get hold of that video?"

"I'd rather not say, Senator. I'm concerned it could put a kid in danger. This doesn't just affect Mr. Martin. There are some thugs on their staff who could turn nasty, especially if it means their jobs."

The senator leaned over and had a short discussion with Bill Rosen. Then, "Bill says we need to know. Maybe you two should talk about it."

"Can we get the kid out of there now?" Brenda realized she had some leverage. They needed that video. So far, nobody had made a move to get it from her. It stayed plugged into her computer.

"Probably we can. I'll get right to work on it Monday." He nodded to John Mallon, who made a few notes.

As the meeting broke up, John came over and sat next to Brenda. "Give me the kid's name."

"Vernal E. Finnegan." She looked over his shoulder. "No, A, A-L. Right."

Tuesday morning she had a phone message from John Mallon. She called immediately. He came on the line.

"About your young friend, Mr. Finnegan. We may have a problem."

"Like what."

"He has a long history of run-ins with authority, including, of course, the law enforcement and judicial kind. Running away from Middleburg twice only compounds the problem."

"But the second time he ran was to give me that video...oops. John, you have to promise me you'll keep that to yourself."

"O.K. I can see how that might boomerang on the kid."

"Thanks. Anyway, that should give him a few points."

"Not necessarily in the eyes of the courts. The other thing, he has no family. What are they supposed to do, send a fourteen-year-old out to seek his fortune -- a fourteen-year-old with the kind of history he's carrying around?"

"Hmm. O.K., suppose he had a family that would take him in, take responsibility for him?" Her mind was working overtime.

"That would help, certainly. Maybe with a strong boost from the senator...."

Monday morning, Brenda called her old classmate Beverly Moses. "Hey, girl, how they treating you down at C. and Y.?"

"Oh, we're fighting off the cuts like everybody else. What's up?"

"You still doing adoptions?"

"Yep. Looks like that's my destiny. I love it. Actually do something for these kids besides move them around the chessboard."

"Got a question. Divorced women can adopt, right?"

"Sho' nuff. You got a client wants to adopt? We got some of the purtiest little babies you ever...."

"I was thinking more of like a fourteen-year-old."

"Oh, hmm. Boy or girl?"

"Boy."

"No father in the picture, right? How about an older male sibling? She got any of those hanging around the house? That age, we'd probably want a guy around. A very stable guy, incidentally."

"I think that can be arranged." Brenda was thinking of Greg Morgan. "Have to be living under the same roof?"

"Oh, you thinking of Big Brothers? Hmm, I guess that would work. It all depends."

"Something like that."

"Have the lady give me a call. What's her name?"

"You're talking to her."

Long pause at the other end of the line. "Brenda, have you lost your...never mind. I think this calls for a little talk, sis. Like over lunch. You owe me one anyway."

Early that afternoon, Brenda and Beverly sat in the cafeteria at County Memorial. Brenda told her friend a little about Flannelmouth and what it would take to get him out of Middleburg.

"O.K.," said Beverly, "I've seen crazier things than that work. You got a boy friend?"

"Nope. Not going there any time soon, either."

"But you got a guy in mind. Tell me about the guy."

Brenda described Greg and how she envisioned Flannelmouth spending time with him volunteering at the Sisters of St. Francis, not to mention trips to ball games and circuses and such.

"White guy, right?" said Beverly. "That might be a little bitty problem. That age, we want somebody the kid can identify with."

"Oh, sorry. Did I neglect to mention that the kid is white?"

"Yes you did. O.K., let's start over. Colored momma gonna adopt a white kid? Irish, I assume."

"Very Irish. He has Irish nightmares."

Beverly was looking at her friend sort of strangely. "Irish nightmares. Tell me, Brenda, what is an Irish nightmare?"

"The man he used to stay with was telling me. While he was growing up, his father, the dear departed Seamus Finnegan, was filling the kid's head full of stories from the old country. Now they fill the kid's dreamtime. I kid you not."

"Got to meet this -- what did you call him, Flannelmouth Finnegan? -- some time. Sounds like a piece of work."

"He's the most lovable kid you could ever hope to meet."

"You're not stringing me along, are you, dear?"

"I swear. I love that kid. I'm serious. He would become one of my own."

Beverly sat thinking about all of this. "O.K., I've heard of crazier things. Not a lot crazier, you understand. But, O.K. You need to get this referred to us. Don't let P. and P. get their hands on it. I can predict right now, they'll try to scotch it. They're into protecting us from the evil teenagers lurking in our streets. Would also have a little problem with the black-white thing."

"Gotcha. O.K., I have to think about this. Lots of pieces to the puzzle."

"Lots. I got just one suggestion: Don't rush it. Too much at stake, friend."

Brenda knew she was right.

Chapter 15.

Home.

There was one individual on whom the whole crazy plan rested -- the one who in a way knew Flannelmouth best.

"Hello, Greg?"

"Hi, any news about Flannelmouth?" Good sign. He really does care about that kid.

"Things are moving. There are a few details still to be worked out, which is one reason I'm calling you."

"O.K., go on."

"I was wondering if you might be interested in a little home cooking -- as in down home."

"As in southern style down home?"

"You got it."

"Sounds interesting. What you have in mind?"

"Dinner at my place Saturday night."

"Oh...well...I've got this...well, O.K. Yeah, I'd like that. What'll I bring?"

"Just bring your appetite."

"O.K. When and where?"

"Six is good. I'm in the big apartment complex at Wilder and Champion -- 1802 Wilder...."

"Hold it, hold it. O.K., 1802 Wilder."

"Right. Main entrance. Pick up the lobby phone and dial me at 512."

"O.K., 512. Got it. I know the general vicinity. Actually not all that far from me. Like fifteen minutes by bus. O.K., see you then. I have your number -- this is

186

your home number, I assume -- in case I have to call you."

"Yes, that's the number. O.K., see you. Bye."

Why was she feeling so elated all of a sudden?

At 6:05 Saturday, the phone rang. Uh oh, prompt type.

"Hi." Hard to read the mood behind Greg's voice.

"Hi. Wait a sec, I'll buzz you in."

When she heard the doorbell, she stopped in front of the mirror long enough to check her hair, then went to let him in. Quick hug in the doorway while he wrestled with a slim paper bag in his hand.

"Hope you like red," he said.

"Come in, come in. Yes, red's fine. Oh, Cabernet. My favorite."

He could see past her into a large living room with a dining area in the rear.

She nodded to the sofa and said, "Make yourself comfortable. Dinner will be just a minute."

He sat gazing around the room while she rattled around in the kitchen. Everything in the place was tastefully done; maybe too tasteful? Not exactly the style section of the Sunday paper, but reasonably close to it. It was a throwback to an earlier time in his life and a world he had abandoned for the austere surroundings at St. Luke's.

A while later they were sitting at the small dining table, candle flames dancing in the glasses of wine.

"Ribs O.K.?" asked Brenda. "They may be a little on the hot and spicy side."

"No, love 'em." He was about to wipe his sticky fingers on the napkin.

"Wait. Let me get some paper napkins. I should have thought of that. We're so used to paper around here," and she was up and off to the kitchen. Greg did a freeze frame while he waited.

"O.K., action, camera," as she dropped a stack of napkins in front of him.

"You said you wanted to talk about Flannelmouth," he said, wiping his hands.

"Yes, Flannelmouth. Wait till I get the rest of the meal," and she went back into the kitchen.

"You said there were a few details to work out," he shouted.

"Wait a minute. It's hard to hear." she called back.

"Can I help?"

"No, that's...yes, I could use some help."

Like everything else in the place, the kitchen was small. He thought of the generous layout in St. Luke's kitchen. Brenda nodded at a sweet potato casserole and a dish of green beans. He started to pick them up, then let go.

"Holders?"

"Oh sorry. In the top drawer there next to the stove."

When he got the dishes to the table, he wondered how everything would fit in the small space.

Brenda came in bearing a plate of fried chicken and a dish of macaroni and cheese.

Greg said, "Quite a feast. We're not expecting to eat all that, I hope."

"Oh, what we don't eat we'll use as leftovers. Tara has a good appetite."

As they ate, they chatted about the meal and the apartment and Brenda's work and her daughter and what was happening with the Sisters of St. Francis and how Greg had knocked around from job to job for ten years after college until he settled on the clergy. It was obvious whom they weren't chatting about.

They were well into the pecan pie when Greg said, "Flannelmouth. You said there were a few details to work out."

Brenda took a long swallow of wine. "Here's the thing. As you know, Flannelmouth does not exactly have a sterling record. He also has no family. That's not a great combination for getting him released from that ashpit."

"Well, so we can't undo those realities. Then it looks like he's stuck there."

"Not exactly. I'll take the family question first. I'm thinking seriously of adopting him."

Greg put down his fork. "Are you serious? In the first place...."

"In the first place, it can be done. I have social work friends in child welfare who can work out the arrangements."

"That's sort of unbelievable. But that takes me to question number two."

"Which is...." Brenda could feel herself gearing up for a fight.

"Question number two is, even if you could pull it off, do you really want to take it on? He's still an adolescent male with a lot of testosterone and, as we know, capable of.... Sorry, skip that."

"No, don't skip that. What were you going to say?" She was trying to keep her cool.

Greg shook his head slightly. "All right, leave that part of it out. Let's assume he's learned his lesson and he's the new Flannelmouth and ready to be a responsible citizen. What about Tara?"

Damn it, he's zeroed right in. She knew what was coming next.

"Has she been consulted about this plan of yours?"

"No."

"Ready for a white guy to join the family household?"

"Uh, I don't know. As I said, there a few details that need to be worked out."

"Sounds like more than a few."

Long silence. "O.K., you're right. Damn you. Damn, damn, damn." So much for the candle light and wine. She didn't want him to see her crying.

"Hey, it's O.K. I didn't mean to upset you," and he grabbed her hand. Now his eyes were getting moist. "It may be a good plan. I think you just have to think it through a little more."

Damn. Sounding like a social worker. She pulled her hand away. "I think you better go."

Greg wasn't ready to go. "There's one more detail."

"What?" She wouldn't look at him.

"Has Flannelmouth been asked what he thinks about all this?"

"Go."

"I...."

"Just go, please."

"O.K. See? I'm walking to the door. See? I'm opening the door. See? I'm out in the hall now." As the door was about to close, he poked his head in. "Thanks for dinner. I really enjoyed it."

She didn't answer. Nor did she get a lot of sleep that night. The trouble was, she knew he was right. Damn.

*

The departure of Mr. Luther Martin from Middleburg was handled discreetly -- as was the arrival of a team of consultants who began holding meetings with staff and inmates and interviewing just about everybody in the place. Several corrections officers were also missing, and in their place were some new, younger men. In short, there was a different feel about the place.

Don Hexley was the new superintendent. He came with a degree in criminal justice from the University of Chicago and experience in running a youth corrections center in the state capital.

Flannelmouth was interviewed twice by consultants. It helped convince him that, if indeed he were stuck in Middleburg, it would be tolerable. Not great, but tolerable.

On Sunday afternoon, came those magic words, "Visitor for you." Flannelmouth was in a good mood as he went to meet with Brenda.

But it wasn't Brenda who was sitting in the meeting room.

"Hi." Greg Morgan waved a hand. He looked thinner and old than Flannelmouth remembered.

"Oh, hi."

"Thought I'd come see if they were treating you all right."

"Yeah. Things are better around here. I...." He searched for words.

"Brenda Jenkins has been trying to figure out a way to get you out of here."

"Yeah, well I.... I'm sorry about, you know...."

"I know the whole story. It's O.K. Actually my life has turned out pretty well."

"They said you left the church.... I mean, you're not a priest any more."

"Right. The good news is they ended up not closing down St. Luke's. They got a young guy leading the flock there. Doing O.K., they say. Don't know how he'd do with the rat patrol." He chuckled, and Flannelmouth managed a smile.

"I've been working at the Sisters of St. Francis. Got a lot going on over there."

"Oh, how are the sisters?"

"They're great. Sister Jennifer and I run the soup kitchen. We got the basketball hoop fixed. Some neat stuff going on with some of the Hispanic and black kids. They're learning to do their fighting shooting baskets instead of guns."

There was so much Flannelmouth wanted to say to the man, but he was stuck in place.

"I...."

"It's O.K., old buddy. You know, you did me a favor. You didn't know that, did you?"

"What do you mean?"

"I should have gotten out of the priesthood a long time ago."

"Huh?"

"I never could really get with the liturgy and ceremonial junk. I always thought Jesus would be one surprised man if he came back and saw what they were doing in His name."

There was a pause, then Flannelmouth said, "You get married to Pamela?"

Greg shook his head with a smile. "When all that other crap happened, it became clear it was a bad match. She was so wrapped up in her world -- actually, herself -- it would never have worked. So I'm still available." He laughed.

Flannelmouth put his face in his hands. "I'm so ashamed."

Greg reached over and put a hand on the trembling shoulder. "It's O.K. You've done a lot of growing up in the last few months. We can't go back and rewrite the script, old buddy. We got to move forward. So what's happening here? I hear there's been a real shakeup."

"That's for sure." Calming down and settling back in his chair, Flannelmouth proceeded to describe in some detail the changes since Old B. and G. left. "I haven't been in solitary once since then," he said proudly.

"Terrific. But we still have to find a way to get you out of here. You got too good stuff to waste it in here." Greg looked at his watch. "I'm going to hit the trail, podner," and he got up to go.

"I'll be back," he added.

"Thanks for coming."

"Thank *you*, friend, I think its been good for both of us."

He walked out, leaving Flannelmouth to ponder it all.

"Hello, Brenda?"

She knew the voice.

"Yes?"

"This is Greg."

"I know."

"I saw Flannelmouth yesterday."

"Oh.... I.... How is he?"

"He seems to be doing fine. Things have really changed there."

"Yes, I know. Was there something you wanted?"

"Actually yes."

She waited.

"You wanted to talk with me about something -- you know, the time you invited me to dinner."

"Oh, yes.... Well I...."

His turn to wait.

"It was about Fannelmouth. People feel he needs more of a connection with a man -- I mean somebody other than the C.O.s and the shrinks. So it's good you went to see him. I think that will help."

"I know it helped me. But was there something more you were thinking of?"

"Well, I.... Well, yes, I'm looking at what happens when he gets out of Middleburg. He's going to need a strong male figure he can identify with."

"You mean spend time with him, a mentor or something like that?"

"Yes, that and going places together. You know...." She realized she hadn't really fleshed out the idea.

"Speaking of all that, any progress on the adoption idea?"

"I thought you'd pretty well quashed that one."

"Oh no, no, not at all. I just felt it needed to be worked out in more detail. I guess we'd agree there are a lot of issues involved."

It took her a moment to respond. "I think I've worked through one. I really do want him to be part of my life. I love that kid. I've also talked to Tara. She was much more accepting than I expected. I guess it's a generation thing.

"And Flannelmouth?"

"I get in to see him just about every weekend. Last weekend was an exception. Glad you went."

It felt like the end of the conversation.

"I did have another reason for calling."

"What?"

"Do you like classical music?"

"Well, I...uh.... As a matter of fact, I was encouraged to study voice; it was a high school music teacher, But I got pregnant and that ended that. Why do you ask?"

"I've got a couple of tickets to the symphony. Well actually it's a dress rehearsal. One heck of a lot cheaper. Thursday evening. Would you be interested in going?"

She tried not to sound too eager. "Yes. Yes, I think that would be nice."

It was the start of something new for both of them. In time it became almost routine. Greg, who thought he knew classical music, had discovered somebody who knew a lot more. For Brenda, dating a white man was uncharted territory.

In the course of things, Greg and Tara got to be friends. There was a kind of banter between them that was outside of Brenda's realm.

"Hey, whitey, that stuff rub off?"

"Sure, but why would I do that? Helps when I walk down a country road in the dark."

"Why white folks talk so funny?"

"It's code. Keeps people guessing."

Sometimes the questions carried a more serious edge. It took Greg a while to learn to stop just shrugging and laughing and settle down instead for some serious talk. Early on, he told her, "Look. I'm a recovering racist -- you know, like a recovering alcholic." He actually found it easier to talk this sort of thing out with Tara than with her mother.

As for Brenda's friends, many of them professional social workers, Greg found the relationship to be accepted a lot more readily than he had expected.

Relationship. They had both veered around that other kind of relationship. It finally came to a head one evening as they were getting back to Brenda's apartment from a movie. Tara was visiting a friend across the river,

"You want to stay over?

He wasn't prepared for it. "You mean...."

In answer she put her arms around him and whispered, "That's exactly what I mean. Come on," and she led him in the direction of her bedroom.

Greg and Brenda had gotten into the habit of Sunday afternoon visits at Middleburg. Flannelmouth looked forward to them all week.

But one question still remained to be answered. The adoption idea had yet to be broached to Flannelmouth. No telling how he'd react.

Greg suggested they talk with the youth together, but Brenda said, "No. This is something I have to do."

That Sunday afternoon as Flannelmouth came into the meeting room, he said, "Oh, Greg's not here? He O.K.?"

"Yes, he's fine. I guess you know we're together now -- I mean we're sharing the apartment."

"I figured as much," said the youth with a smile.

"My daughter Tara's moving out soon, which means there will be an extra room at the apartment. How would you feel about moving in there, you know, live in the apartment with us?"

"That would be fantastic, Brenda, but...." He motioned toward the wall with his head. "Guess I'm stuck here."

"Not necessarily. There's another piece to this."

"What do you mean?"

"Do you know anything about adoption?"

"Sure. They adopted my baby sister out and we never heard from her again."

"They don't just adopt babies. They adopt people older than that, like fourteen year olds for example."

It took Flannelmouth a moment to grasp what she was saying.

"You mean...?"

"I'm prepared to adopt you, my dear. For you to become family in a literal sense. We still have to get permission from the state, but it looks like it can be arranged."

"Would you be, like, my mother?"

She nodded.

"Would Greg be my father?"

"That remains to be seen. Right now we're not talking marriage, but who knows? Stranger things have happened. Keep you posted."

They stood in the middle of the floor in a prolonged hug. Flannelmouth mumbled something.

"What did you say?"

"I said I vote yes -- on the marriage thing, I mean."

And so it was that on a particularly sunny and hot day in April, a bright-eyed fifteen-year-old walked out of the Middleburg Juvenile Training Center for the last time. He spotted two familiar figures up at the gate.

Flannelmouth ran into their open arms. Brenda and Greg were both weeping openly as the three of them clung together for several minutes.

"Time to go home," said Brenda.

"Time to go home," said Greg.

All the lad could do was hold on tight and nod.

The end.

24269684R00111

Made in the USA
Charleston, SC
18 November 2013